DATE DUE

MAY 0 2 P.M.			
MAY 2 3 1991			
MAY 2 6 1992			

F
Mil   Mills, Claudia
         Dynamite Dinah

Dynamite DINAH

Dynamite DINAH

CLAUDIA MILLS

Macmillan Publishing Company
New York

Collier Macmillan Publishers
London

The poem "Renascence" is reprinted from
The Collected Poems of Edna St. Vincent Millay
by arrangement.

Macmillan Publishing Company
866 Third Avenue, New York, NY 10022
Collier Macmillan Canada, Inc.
Printed in the United States of America

10 9 8 7 6 5 4 3 2

The text of this book is set in 12 point Sabon.
Library of Congress Cataloging-in-Publication Data
Mills, Claudia. Dynamite Dinah / Claudia Mills.—1st ed.   p.   cm.
Summary: Mischievous Dinah struggles to remain the center of
attention when her baby brother comes home from the hospital and
her best friend gets a lead role in the class play.
ISBN 0-02-767101-1
[1. Behavior—Fiction.   2. Friendship—Fiction.
3. Schools—Fiction.   4. Babies—Fiction.]   I. Title.
PZ7.M63963Dy   1990   [Fic]—dc20
89-13300   CIP   AC

For the buzzin' cousins:
Richelle, Natalie, and Samantha

One

_____

It was the first day of March, and the world looked like winter, but smelled like spring. The trees were bare, and the lawns were littered with shrinking patches of dirty snow, but the wind that sent the dead leaves scuttling along the sidewalks was warm and buoyant. Kite-flying weather, except that the sky was overcast and the radio had forecast rain.

Dinah Seabrooke turned to walk backward. The wind caught her full in the face, buffeting her eyelashes and lifting her thick tangle of frizzy brown curls off her shoulders. The first line of a poem popped into her head: *If I were a kite in a windy sky*. Dinah was good at thinking of first lines of poems. It was harder to think of second lines, and third, and fourth. But she wrote down the first lines, anyway, when she remembered them. Maybe someday they could be published all together in a big book: *First Lines*, by Dinah Seabrooke, age ten. It might be a best-seller, and then Dinah would be on all the television talk shows.

Dinah's best friend, Suzanne Kelly, was waiting with the other fifth graders on the blacktop behind Riverdale Elementary School.

"Isn't it a wonderful day?" Dinah asked her, breathless from walking against the wind. She stuck out her tongue to catch one of the big fat raindrops that had begun to splatter on the pavement.

"No," Suzanne said patiently. "It's going to rain. It *is* raining."

"I know, but don't you love rain?"

"No. I don't even *like* rain."

Across the playground, Artie Adams, who always knew everything before anyone else did, called to them, "Guess who has a substitute?" His wide grin gave the answer away.

"*Now* don't you think it's a wonderful day?" Not that Dinah had anything personal against Mrs. Hall, their regular teacher. But with a substitute she had a sense of boundless possibility. The odds were better that something interesting would happen. Or, rather, that Dinah could make something interesting happen.

"I have an idea," she said.

Suzanne groaned good-naturedly.

"When she calls the roll, how about I'll answer for your name, and you answer for mine. And then all day long I can pretend to be you, and you can pretend to be me."

The rain was falling in earnest now. One of the playground aides opened the school doors; in bad weather the children could come inside before the first bell.

"Okay?" Dinah asked, nudging Suzanne with her unopened umbrella.

"You're a nut, did you know that?" Suzanne asked. But she didn't say no, and Dinah took that for yes.

In Room 5A, a plump grandmotherly woman with curly gray hair was sitting at Mrs. Hall's desk. She looked as if she had just taken off her apron after baking a few dozen oatmeal raisin cookies. On the board her name was spelled out in neat cursive writing: Mrs. Overton.

Following the flag salute, Mrs. Overton opened the worn black attendance book that Mrs. Hall kept in her top desk drawer. "You're going to have to help me with your names, boys and girls," she told the class. "Let me know if I mispronounce anything, or if there's a nickname you prefer."

Dinah felt a pleasant surge of anticipation. She liked helping substitute teachers with her name. One time she had told a substitute that her nickname was Dynamite. Another time she had insisted that her last name was pronounced Sea-brook-ee. The Dynamite sub hadn't believed her, but the other sub had called her "Miss Seabrookee" for half the morning.

"Irving Adams," Mrs. Overton read from the top of the list.

"Artie," he corrected her. "From my middle name, Arthur." As often as the class had heard this, the general mirth could not be contained.

"Ir-ving!" Nathan Daniels sang out. "Ir-ving!" A wave of giggles swept the room.

Mrs. Overton pronounced Andy Feinstein's name as Fine-stine instead of Fine-steen, provoking more titters.

Then: "Suzanne Kelly."

"Here," Dinah called quickly, before Suzanne could change her mind.

Caught by surprise, the rest of the class showed no reaction. But a moment later, when Suzanne answered for Dinah, the laughter made Mrs. Overton look up from the roll book.

"Dinah Seabrooke," she repeated. "Did I pronounce it wrong? Or do you have a nickname?"

"Um—no," Suzanne managed to say, once she realized that Mrs. Overton was still talking to her.

"All right, then," Mrs. Overton said.

When the last name had been called, Mrs. Overton asked, "Who would like to take the attendance cards down to the office?" Every hand went up. Dinah didn't care particularly whether she was picked or not, but her good mood made her feel like hamming it up. She waved her whole arm so vigorously, flinging it back and forth with all her might, that she almost fell out of her chair.

"Suzanne, you may go," Mrs. Overton decided. Dinah collapsed back into her seat, miming disappointment, and then remembered: *She* was Suzanne! From the back of the room someone snorted as she bounded up to Mrs. Overton's desk to collect her prize, but Mrs. Overton didn't seem to notice.

Outside in the silent, deserted hallway, Dinah hugged herself with happiness. The day was turning out so nicely.

As she was making her way along the main hallway on the first floor, she saw the janitor's mop and bucket by the front door, where the students had left muddy footprints. At the same time two fourth graders appeared, carrying the attendance cards for their rooms. The combination of prop and audience was irresistible.

Still clutching the attendance cards in one hand, Dinah lifted the heavy mop from the bucket and began busily swishing it across the black and white tiles of the hallway floor. The wet tiles gleamed like ebony and ivory. The fourth graders stopped walking to watch. For good measure, Dinah added what she hoped was a waltz step, in time to "Waltzing Matilda." Holding the mop as her partner, she swooped and glided: "Waltzing Matilda! Waltzing Matilda! You'll come a-waltzing, Matilda, with me!"

Savoring the rapt attention of the fourth-grade couriers, Dinah didn't hear Pop Fody approaching until it was too late.

"Keepa your hands off!" he yelled. Pop Fody didn't really have an accent, but he liked to use one when he talked to kids.

Startled, Dinah slipped on the wet tiles that she had

LOUISE WHITE SCHOOL

just finished mopping. The mop handle went crashing, narrowly missing the heads of her still-fascinated audience.

"What do you think you're doing?" Pop Fody wanted to know.

"I'm taking the attendance cards to the office," Dinah replied haughtily, as if the answer should be perfectly obvious to any reasonable person. But where were the attendance cards? She had had them a minute ago. Dinah glanced around her and, horrified, saw the cards for Room 5A floating on the surface of the dark greasy water in Pop Fody's bucket. Pop saw them, too, and raised the bushy black eyebrows that matched his bushy black mustache.

"I dropped them, that's all," Dinah said. "A person can drop things, you know."

"I'll drop *you*, next time I see you messing with my mop."

Another poetic fragment leaped out at Dinah:

> "Don't mess with my mop,"
> Said Pop.

But this was no time for poetry. As the fourth graders continued to watch, Dinah fished the dripping attendance cards from the water and tried patting them dry against her skirt. They definitely needed more than patting. Maybe she could dry them under the blowers in the girls' room.

"Get along with you." Pop gestured toward the office.

"Um—I have to go to the girls' room."

"Git!" Pop roared.

Dinah got.

In the office Mrs. Burns, the school secretary, stared at the soggy attendance cards in despair. "What on earth happened to them? Did you take them outside in the rain?"

"I dropped them." It was tiring to have to keep giving the same explanation over and over again.

"You *dropped* them? Dropped them *where*?"

"In Pop Fody's bucket." Dinah thought quickly. "It was in the middle of the hall. Where anybody could trip over it."

"And *you* tripped over it?"

"Sort of." The less said about "Waltzing Matilda," the better.

Mrs. Burns gave up. "All right, get on back to class. And no dawdling."

Dinah gave her a look as if to say, *What? Me? Dawdle?* But in fact she hurried upstairs to her class.

"There you are, Suzanne," Mrs. Overton greeted her. "We were beginning to worry."

"Here I am!" Dinah said brightly.

"Does it always take this long to go to the office and back?"

"Um—sometimes it takes longer than others." That much was true. Dinah opened her math book to the same page as Suzanne's and pretended to be absorbed by how to divide fractions. Mrs. Overton was about to say something else when Mr. Saganario, the principal, peered through the square window in the classroom door.

"Excuse me, boys and girls," Mrs. Overton said, and bustled out into the hall to see what he wanted.

Enough of fractions. Dinah laid down her math book and, from her desk next to the window, gazed out at the rain. Room 5A was on the second floor, overlooking the flat roof of the one-story addition to the school that had been built a few years before. The rain was drumming fiercely on the roof. A gust of wind sent a torrent of water against the window, as if a giant janitor's bucket had been knocked over somewhere in the dark, seething sky.

Dinah left her seat and perched on the broad windowsill. She pressed her face against the cold glass, all that separated her from the storm. Grunting with the effort—the classroom windows always stuck—she raised the sash a few inches and thrust her hands outside to feel the rain on her bare skin. Then she forced the window open wide enough so that she could poke her head out, too. The wind and the rain beat against her upturned face and lashed at her hair.

The roof stretched before her. If Dinah sat on the ledge with her feet dangling out the window, the tips of her loafers would just graze the cement. She began repositioning herself, glad that Mr. Saganario was so long-winded.

"Dinah's going to climb out the window!" Artie called, loudly enough that everyone looked up from the math work sheets, but not loudly enough to be overheard in the corridor.

Was she going to climb out the window? It would be a shame not to, with the wild rain beckoning and all eyes upon her. Feeling like a tightrope walker under the big top, drums rolling and the crowd hushed in anticipation, Dinah slipped out onto the roof.

Dinah wished she could do an elaborate song-and-dance routine, like Gene Kelly in *Singin' in the Rain*, one of her parents' favorite old movies. Instead she made up a dance of her own to the same music, the dance of a leaf blown hither and yon, of a raindrop flung against the glass, of a kite in a windy sky. It was wonderful to be outside dancing instead of inside watching. It seemed so boring to be safe and dry.

Boring or not, however, Dinah knew that the rest of her life would be more pleasant if she was back in her seat by the time Mrs. Overton returned to the room. She ended the dance with a hasty flourish and hurried across the roof to the open window. But the window was open no longer. Grinning at her through the glass, Artie Adams was holding it shut.

"Let me in!" Dinah shouted.

Artie kept on grinning.

Alarmed now, Dinah dashed to the next window, but Artie was as quick as she was. Dinah tried to raise it up; with equal strength, Artie held it down.

At that moment Mrs. Overton reappeared. "Irving!" she called. "I mean, Arthur! I mean, Artie! Come away from that window *now*!"

Mrs. Overton strode across the room, less like a cookie-baking grandma than the general of an advancing army. With a mighty heave, she raised the window and Dinah scrambled back inside.

"What is the meaning of this?" Mrs. Overton demanded. "Out on the roof! In this weather! I think you'd better go down to Mr. Saganario's office, Suzanne. And I'm going to leave a note for Mrs. Hall so she can take this behavior into account when she marks your report card. I'm going to have to tell her that Suzanne Kelly is a very disruptive young lady."

Dinah gulped. She had forgotten the name switch.

"Actually," she said, "Suzanne Kelly isn't disruptive at all."

Mrs. Overton glared at her. "I think I had better be the judge of that."

"No, I mean, I'm not Suzanne Kelly. *She's* Suzanne Kelly. I'm Dinah Seabrooke."

"Oh, you are, are you. Well, aren't we full of jokes this morning. Now off to the principal's office with you before you catch your death of cold."

Soaked through and beginning to shiver, Dinah made her exit from Room 5A. This was not the first time she had been sent to Mr. Saganario's office. Or the second. Or the third.

Mr. Saganario just shook his head when Dinah appeared before him, huddled inside the blanket the school nurse had brought. "Dancing. On the rooftop. In the rain." He scribbled notes on his blotter. "Don't you think we've had quite enough this year of incidents of this kind?"

Incidents of *what* kind? Dinah had never been sent to the principal before for anything that had to do with dancing or rooftops or rain. The other incidents, as she remembered them fondly, had involved bananas and scissors and colored chalk.

"I guess so," Dinah said, because she had learned from experience that it saved time and effort to give Mr. Saganario the answer he wanted. But she couldn't help thinking that "incidents of this kind" were what made life interesting, gave it its special magic. A week of detention seemed a small price to pay for five minutes of dancing on the rooftop in the rain.

Two

The school nurse called Dinah's mother for a change of clothes, and Mrs. Seabrooke arrived at school with them ten minutes later.

"Dinah," her mother said reproachfully, as Dinah began pulling off her damp clothes and donning the dry ones. "What am I going to do with you? Don't you ever think? What if you had fallen off?"

"It wasn't that kind of roof," Dinah reassured her. "And I was about a mile from the edge."

"Suppose you come down with pneumonia?"

"I won't. I won't even get a cold. I won't even get a sniffle." Dinah was warming to her topic. "I won't give a single sneeze. I won't blow my nose once—"

"That we shall see," Mrs. Seabrooke interrupted. "But, really, Dinah, don't you think I have enough to do with clients waiting and Benjamin due to arrive any day? Any minute? You're lucky that I try to schedule my appointments with some slack in between for unexpected delays. But enough is enough. It's not fair to expect me to drop everything and rush over here with a dry outfit just because you feel like going out in the rain."

"The dry clothes weren't my idea. I didn't mind the wet ones, and I told Mrs. Riley not to bother you, but she went ahead and called, anyway." Tears sprang into Dinah's eyes. She hadn't meant to make work for her mother. And her rain-drenched clothes were practically dry already.

Mrs. Seabrooke gave Dinah a quick hug. "Just try to be a little more considerate next time, okay?"

Dinah hugged her mother back, as tightly as she could with her mother's huge, enormous, stupendous belly in the way. Her mother was the fattest woman Dinah had ever seen, but it was all right: She wasn't really fat, just pregnant. After ten years of being an only child, Dinah was going to have a baby brother, Benjamin.

In books she had read, somebody's mother would be mysteriously sick, and the next day the "sickness" would turn out to be a baby brother or sister. Such stories now seemed preposterous to Dinah. How could you not know that your own mother was going to have a baby? Even if Dinah could have been blind to her mother's bulging figure, she could hardly have ignored all the preparations that had consumed her parents' attention in the past nine months. They were even going to special classes to learn how to have a baby. Dinah's father, who had been out at sea in the Navy when Dinah was born, was going to help with the birth this time, so he went to the classes with Dinah's mother and read book after book on different childbirth methods.

But even more than books on childbirth, Dinah's parents were reading books on sibling rivalry. Dinah saw the books on the coffee table, opened to the sections on "Problems with the School-Age Child." Everyone seemed to assume that Dinah was going to mind having a baby brother. She overheard people asking her parents in a worried whisper, "How is Dinah taking the news?" or saying, "I hope you're not going to have problems with Dinah."

Didn't they know that Dinah wanted a baby brother or sister more than anything in the world? For years, before she had known better, she had put A NEW BABY, underlined and in capital letters, at the very top of her Christmas wish list. It was lonely being an only child. It was like being a stand-up comedian in front of an empty theater, telling joke after joke with nobody to laugh, nobody even to hiss or boo. One of Dinah's teachers had told them that a tree falling in a forest makes no sound if there is no one there to hear it. On rainy weekend afternoons, while her parents were catching up on their reading, Dinah understood how the tree in the forest must feel. She had made a sign for her bedroom door that said GENIUS AT WORK — EMPLOYEES ONLY. But the trouble was that Dinah had no employees, no one to run and sharpen pencils for her while her genius simmered.

Now she would have Benjamin. He would be too small at first, of course, to laugh at Dinah's jokes or sharpen her pencils. But in time, with the proper training . . . No, Dinah could hardly wait for Benjamin's arrival. She had been waiting too many years already.

"Do you think you can stay out of trouble for the rest of the day?" Dinah's mother asked. She gathered up Dinah's wet clothes and turned to go. "Or better yet, for the rest of the year?"

Dinah seriously doubted it. But her mother, who never looked tired, looked tired now. "I'll try," she promised, and she even meant it. "I really will try."

———

"So what happened?" Artie asked Dinah as they stood side by side in the lunch line.

"Nothing." It was pigs-in-blankets day, and Dinah loved pigs-in-blankets.

"I mean, what did they do to you?" Artie's face lit up with anticipation.

"Nothing," Dinah repeated.

The answer visibly struck a death blow to Artie's hopes. "Nothing? You climbed out on the *roof* and they did *nothing*?"

"Oh, I got detention. For a week. And they called my mother."

Artie looked somewhat relieved, but still not fully satisfied. It was so plain that the punishments didn't bother Dinah in the slightest.

"That's *all*?"

"Pretty much. Mr. Saganario said he's going to put it in my Permanent Record." This was the principal's favorite threat, but it didn't work as intended on Dinah. She was pleased to think that her exploits were documented for posterity. She was proud that her Permanent Record, unlike most people's, would make fascinating reading for future generations of school principals. It could even be made into a movie: *The Permanent Record of Dinah Seabrooke.*

"Didn't your mom get mad?" Artie asked. "Mine would have had a conniption fit."

Dinah chose a vanilla and chocolate ice-cream cup for dessert and set it on her tray. "Not really." It was true. Her mother never got mad. Exasperated, sometimes. Irritated. Annoyed. But never really angry.

"I saw her from the window when she came in. She looks like she's going to have quintuplets, or something."

"Well, it's not quintuplets. Nowadays they know."

"Sometimes they do, and sometimes they don't," Artie said. "But I've had two baby sisters, and I can tell you one thing: Your mom's not going to be that easy to get along with anymore. Not for a long time. Not by a long shot."

———

After detention Dinah went to the public library. The

rain had stopped, and the bright blue sky looked freshly scrubbed, with only a few puffy clouds around the edges, like stray soapsuds.

"How can we help you today, Dinah?" Mrs. Jacob, the children's librarian, asked.

"I need to find a poem."

"Any poem in particular?" Mrs. Jacob liked finding things for people.

"Sort of. I want to find the longest poem in the world."

"Let me guess. Mrs. Hall wants everyone to memorize a poem to recite in class, and you're here to pick yours."

"How did you know?" Sure enough, Mrs. Hall had made the assignment the day before.

Mrs. Jacob laughed. "Artie Adams was in here yesterday, looking for the *shortest* poem in the world."

Dinah mentally eliminated Artie as one potential source of competition. She had her heart set on reciting a poem that was longer than anyone else's.

"The longest poem in the world," Mrs. Jacob said thoughtfully. "There are a lot of extremely long poems, Dinah. Many whole books have been written as poetry—the *Iliad* and the *Odyssey* of Homer, for example, or Tennyson's *Idylls of the King*. Those would take you years to memorize. So let's see what else we can find, all right?"

She led Dinah to the poetry shelves and began pulling down anthologies for her to browse through, talking all the while. " 'Casey at the Bat' is a nice long one. Or 'The Cremation of Sam McGee.' Here's 'The Highwayman,' a classic. Oh, and here's one I loved when I was a girl, 'Renascence,' by Edna St. Vincent Millay. She wrote it when she was just nineteen."

Dinah began to read "Renascence," and from the first lines she knew she had found her poem. No one knew the importance of first lines better than Dinah, and these were simple and direct, leading her on into the heart of the poem:

> All I could see from where I stood
> Was three long mountains and a wood;
> I turned and looked another way,
> And saw three islands in a bay.

And the poem was long! It went on for page after page, two hundred lines in all. But Dinah would have wanted to memorize "Renascence" even if it hadn't been practically guaranteed to be the longest poem memorized by anyone in Room 5A, maybe longer than everybody else's poems put together. The poem told the story of a girl who dies and lies buried in the grave, never more to see, hear, smell, taste, sense anything on earth. And then, miraculously, her life is given back to her, to live more fully than before, for now she knows what it would be like to lose it. The poem soared to a burst of rapture that made Dinah's heart swell:

> Ah! Up then from the ground sprang I
> And hailed the earth with such a cry
> As is not heard save from a man
> Who has been dead, and lives again.
> About the trees my arms I wound;

Like one gone mad I hugged the ground
I raised my quivering arms on high;
I laughed and laughed into the sky . . .

Edna St. Vincent Millay would have climbed out the window and danced in the rain, too.

———

When Dinah reached home, the house was empty, but she was used to looking after herself in the afternoon. Her father managed a sporting-goods store; he worked till six, and some evenings, too. Dinah's mother had her own business, one she had created herself. She was an "organization consultant." Disorganized people hired her, and she helped them to become more organized. She organized closets, checkbooks, menus, weddings, holiday celebrations, attics, whole lives. The Seabrooke family was, appropriately, the most organized family Dinah had ever seen.

Dinah's father wasn't as organized as Dinah's mother, but he didn't mind having his shirts hung by color in his closet and his socks neatly arrayed in a special sock caddy. Every once in a while, though, he had a small surge of rebellion against his wife's lists and schedules. He liked to tease, so he'd make comical entries on the weekly grocery list or drive Dinah's mother crazy by leaving one of the kitchen drawers open half an inch.

It was Dinah's job, when she arrived home from school, to check the list posted on the refrigerator, which told the menu for each night's dinner and what she could do to start preparing it. MONDAY, the list would say.

Honey baked chicken, wild rice, broccoli. Dinah, please turn over the chicken pieces in the marinade. Or: TUESDAY. *Beef stew. Dinah, please take from fridge at 4:00 and put on simmer.*

Today was Thursday: *Leftover beef stew. I'll microwave when I get home.* But also taped to the refrigerator door was a large sheet of construction paper, bearing a hastily scrawled message in Magic Marker: "BABY B IS ON HIS WAY!"

Without grabbing her jacket, Dinah ran outside, too excited to stay at home another minute. It was a beautiful day to be born on. *Benjamin, Benjamin, Benjamin!* Her feet pounded the rhythm on the pavement as she ran the three blocks to Suzanne's house, where she was to stay while her parents were at the hospital. *Benjamin, Benjamin, Benjamin!*

Mrs. Kelly opened the door before Dinah could ring the bell, her smile almost as broad as Dinah's.

"I know," she said. "Your mother called me."

The Kellys were a big family. Suzanne was the youngest, with a brother and sister who were away at college and a brother in high school. Dinah loved visiting their rambling, comfortable house, and the Kellys always made a fuss over her.

"Dynamite!" Suzanne's fifteen-year-old brother, Tom, greeted her now. He had called her that ever since Dinah had told him how she had tried out her self-chosen nickname on a substitute back in third grade. "So you're going to have a kid brother any minute!"

Dinah beamed. Tom was one of her favorite people.

Secretly she had decided that she wouldn't mind marrying him someday if she had to marry somebody.

"I heard you got pretty wet this morning," he said.

It was all the encouragement Dinah needed to launch into the story. Dinah liked telling stories about her adventures even more than she liked having adventures in the first place. She talked fast—she could recite the Gettysburg Address in sixty seconds, even faster than Abraham Lincoln. Her voice rose and fell to heighten the drama of what she was telling. She talked with her hands, her face, her whole body.

When she got to the part where Artie Adams was holding the window shut, Tom began laughing. He kept on chuckling through the tale of Dinah's confrontation with the principal.

"One more for the Permanent Record," he said.

The phone rang. Dinah's heart jumped.

"Go ahead, answer it," Tom told her.

Dinah grabbed the receiver. "Kelly residence," she managed to say.

"Dinah! It's Daddy, at the hospital. You have a baby brother!"

Three

After supper the next day, Dinah's father drove her to the hospital for the sibling visiting hour.

"Now, you can't expect Benjamin to look like a baby in a baby-food commercial," Mr. Seabrooke warned her as he backed the car into the last empty space in the crowded hospital parking lot. "Being born's hard work, and Benjamin hasn't even had twenty-four hours to recover from it."

"Does he look like I did when I was a baby?"

"He looks like himself, and you looked like yourself," Mr. Seabrooke said, as if to head off any comparisons. It sounded like a line he might have learned from the sibling-rivalry books. "You were a beautiful baby, and Benjamin is, too."

Dinah didn't care how beautiful she had been, but she hoped she had been a baby with some character and spunk. She tried to picture a miniature version of her present self—an infant dynamo whose antics were both the delight and despair of the hospital staff.

The maternity ward and nursery were on the third floor. Dinah and her father stopped at the nursing station there to find out where they were supposed to go.

"First let's get you scrubbed up," the nurse said, returning Dinah's smile. She led them to a small room with a white porcelain sink. "I want you to wash your hands for three whole minutes. Here's surgical soap and a sterile sponge. Ready? One, two, three, scrub!"

Three minutes is a very short time to talk on the telephone or watch TV, but a very long time to wash hands. Dinah scrubbed hers until every last, lingering germ had surely been rinsed away, and still the big clock above the sink told her that she had two minutes more of scrubbing left to go. Rub-a-dub-dub! Scrub, scrub, scrub! She kept on scrubbing until the backs of her hands were red and tingling. Then the nurse gave her a cotton hospital gown to put on over her clothes.

Once she had tied the gown at the neck and waist, Dinah studied herself in the full-length mirror hung on the wall next to the sink. She looked important, like a patient on a soap opera about to undergo brain surgery.

She pretended that she had already had brain surgery. Pale and wan, she had just come out of a ten-hour operation to cure a rare disease of the brain. But she needed bandages on her head, lots of them. Aha! There was a big stack of white hospital towels in a cart parked next to the sink.

As she finished wrapping one around her head, turban-style, her father was tying on his own hospital gown. Mr. Seabrooke usually enjoyed Dinah's comedy routines, but today he seemed in a hurry. "Let's not clown around, Dinah," he said, with hardly a glance at her bandaged brain. "Your mother and Benjamin are waiting."

Off came the towel, but Dinah felt annoyed. Suppose she had really had a ten-hour brain operation. Would he be rushing her along then, too? But of course she hadn't. As eager to see Benjamin as he was, she followed her father back to the nursing station and then down the hall to the sibling visiting room. There in a wheelchair sat her mother, wearing a hospital gown of her own. And beside her, in a clear plastic bassinet on wheels, was baby Benjamin.

"Ohhh!" Dinah whispered.

He was so small! Swaddled tightly in a lightweight receiving blanket, he looked like a little blue inchworm. Only his head stuck out at the top. He was fast asleep.

"Do you want to hold him?" Dinah's mother asked.

Wordlessly, Dinah nodded. Her father leaned over the bassinet and gathered up the little blue bundle. Then he laid Benjamin in Dinah's arms. With the tip of her thoroughly scrubbed forefinger, Dinah touched Benjamin's nose, and his ears, and the little indentation in his chin.

"What do you think?" Mr. Seabrooke asked. "Should we keep him?"

"Does he know I'm holding him? Will he smile?"

"He can't smile yet," Dinah's mother said. "It'll be another month or two before that happens."

Dinah felt a pang of disappointment. She had wanted their first meeting to be as momentous for Benjamin as it was for her, but not only was he not going to smile —he might even sleep through the whole thing.

"Give him time, Dinah," her father said. "Before you know it, he'll be more fun than a barrel full of monkeys."

Dinah touched Benjamin's tiny button nose again and then let her father take him. Benjamin wasn't required to be all *that* much fun. Two barrels full of monkeys in one family might be one barrel too many. But she wished he'd smile or laugh, at least give one small chortle or chuckle. Didn't he care that of all the ten-year-old girls in the world, he had Dynamite Dinah as his very own big sister?

———

Because Benjamin had ended up being born by a Cesarean delivery, Dinah's mother had to stay in the hospital for five days. Dinah went to the hospital to visit once more over the weekend, but Benjamin seemed no happier to see her than he had the first time. Less happy, even. The first time he had slept; this time he cried and howled and wailed.

"How come he can't smile for two months, but he can cry right away?" Dinah wanted to know. "It'd be a lot better if it was the other way around."

"I'll say!" said her mother.

"Maybe he's just crying because he doesn't like the hospital," Dinah suggested. "I bet you'll stop crying as soon as you get home, won't you, Benjamin?"

"There's something to that," Mrs. Seabrooke said. "Here I feed Benjamin at two A.M. one night, four o'clock the next, whenever they bring him to me. That kind of unpredictability is upsetting, for him and for me. Once we get him on a schedule, settled into a routine, life's bound to be easier for all of us."

Mr. Seabrooke, who had been pacing back and forth with Benjamin held high against his shoulder, tried rocking him in his lap, to no avail. Benjamin's cries continued unabated.

"Schedule, eh?" Dinah's father asked. "Routine? I don't know, Judy. I'm not sure Benjamin here's going to be your most cooperative client."

"Babies love schedules," Dinah's mother insisted. "Dinah did."

"What do you say, Benjamin?" Mr. Seabrooke asked. "Are you going to be the most organized baby ever?"

For answer, Benjamin kept on howling.

———

Before she left for school on Tuesday, Dinah hung the sign she had made over the living-room fireplace:
WELCOME HOME, BENJAMIN!
Benjamin was a long name, so she had had to write the last part of it in smaller and smaller letters to make it fit her piece of red construction paper.

It was a typical school day, with many exciting adventures and escapades. And all day long Dinah knew that when she got home, Benjamin would be there! She fidgeted and squirmed through detention, until Mrs. Burns threatened her with an extra day if she couldn't keep still. The instant she was free, Dinah ran all the way home, eager to tell her parents and Benjamin her biggest and best stories.

The next few weeks were going to be special ones. Dinah's mother had arranged her schedule so she'd have several uninterrupted months of maternity leave, with no disorganized clients to attend to, and her father was trying to cut back as much as possible on his hours at the store. No more coming home to an empty house with dinner instructions posted on the refrigerator! Instead there'd be the smell of dinner already simmering on the stove, and *two* parents plus one brand-new baby brother waiting to ask Dinah the question that was music to her ears: "How was school today?"

But when she burst into the front hallway and slammed her backpack on the floor, her father hurried up to her with his finger on his lips.

"Try to keep the noise down, honey. We just put Benjamin down for a nap, and we're hoping he'll sleep a decent stretch this time."

"Where's Mom?" Dinah asked in a whisper.

"She's taking a nap, too. Or trying to."

Sleeping in the middle of the afternoon! Dinah had never heard of such a thing. Her mother had always maintained that a brisk walk was more refreshing than a nap any day.

Dinah sniffed the air expectantly, but caught no pleasing aroma of cooking. "What's for dinner?"

"Dinner?" Her father seemed puzzled. "Oh, dinner. The Kellys are bringing something over, I think."

So far her father hadn't asked her about school, but Dinah knew he was momentarily distracted by Benjamin. The first day with a new baby in the house was bound to be a little bit hectic.

"Guess what?" she asked. Many of Dinah's stories began that way. She didn't really expect the other person to offer any guesses. It was her way of alerting her audience to the fact that they were about to hear something very interesting.

"What?" her father asked automatically.

"We had an eating contest in school today. At lunch."

An eating contest! her father was supposed to say. *Eating what? Were you part of it? Who won?*

"That's nice," he said.

Nice? But Dinah wasn't easily discouraged.

"Well, it was sort of a contest. More like a dare, really. I said I was hungry enough to eat fifty Dixie cups. You know, of ice cream. Chocolate on one side and vanilla on the other side. Well, Artie Adams heard me, and he said—"

"You know, I might stretch out myself, just for a few minutes," her father said. "I have a feeling we're in for a long night."

"Don't you want to know what happened next? How

Artie Adams said, 'I bet you can't eat fifty Dixie cups,' and I said, 'I can, too,' and then—"

"Save it for dinner, okay, honey? I really want to hear all about it, but right now it's hard for me to concentrate. Either your mother and I have forgotten a lot about babies, or else we're ten years older than we were the last time around. Or both."

"Okay," Dinah said. Her story would keep, for a little while at least.

Still stuffed from the eating contest, Dinah decided against an afternoon snack and settled herself on the living-room couch with her copy of "Renascence" to memorize. "All I could see from where I stood / Was three long mountains and a wood." She read the words out loud, then closed her eyes and repeated them under her breath. Two lines learned, one hundred ninety-eight to go. "I turned and looked another way, / And saw three islands in a bay."

She was muttering the thirty-ninth and fortieth lines to herself when her mother came into the room.

"Mom!" Dinah sprang up from the couch and ran over for a kiss. She hadn't realized how much she had missed her mother until she felt how wonderful it was to have her home again. Her father had a better sense of humor, and he appreciated Dinah's clowning more. But it was her mother who gave Dinah the feeling that all was right with the world.

"How was school?" her mother asked, but before Dinah could answer, the doorbell rang. It was Mr. Kelly and Tom, with two enormous hampers of food.

"The hot food is still hot, in case you'd like to start in on it right away," Mr. Kelly said. "There's meat loaf, ratatouille, buttered noodles, green beans amandine, and some rolls. Tom has the cold things—your salad and chocolate mousse cake."

Dinah began to wish she hadn't eaten quite so many Dixie cups.

"Oh, and the chilled bottle of champagne."

Mrs. Seabrooke shook her head in wonder. "When Jane offered to make dinner, I never dreamed she'd cater us a feast. This is enough food for a week."

With a friendly wink to Dinah, Mr. Kelly began unpacking the two hampers. He was a quiet, gentle man, unperturbed through any commotion.

Tom helped Dinah set the table. "How's your appetite, Dinah?" he asked as he set a paper napkin by each plate. "I heard you had a few extra helpings of ice cream at lunch today."

"Only fourteen," Dinah said, relieved at being able to tell her story at last. "It was supposed to be fifty. You see, I was hungry right before lunch, really hungry. And I told Suzanne I could eat fifty Dixie cups. And Artie Adams was right behind us in line, and *he* said—"

"Go call your father, honey," Dinah's mother interrupted. "I don't know how to thank Jane."

"Just enjoy your first dinner home," Mr. Kelly said. "Now, don't let us intrude any longer on your special evening."

The Kellys collected the empty hampers, and then they were gone. Tom never had a chance to find out what

Artie Adams had said and how it had triggered the great Riverdale School eating extravaganza.

Dinah's father was as amazed by Mrs. Kelly's dinner as Dinah's mother had been.

"Whatever else happens, we won't starve," he said.

Mrs. Seabrooke began serving steaming slices of meatloaf smothered in ratatouille sauce, and Mr. Seabrooke popped the cork on the champagne.

"Pass me your glass, Dinah. We'll give you a taste of the bubbly, too." He poured a sip of champagne into Dinah's glass and filled the others to the brim.

"A toast!" he proposed.

Feeling worldly and sophisticated, Dinah raised her glass in imitation of her parents.

"To good friends, good food, and most of all, to Benjamin!"

As if on cue, a piteous wail rose from the nursery.

"Oh, no!" Mrs. Seabrooke said, half laughing, half crying. "I did so want to enjoy Jane's dinner."

"I'll get him." Mr. Seabrooke bounded up from the table, his plate untouched. "Go ahead and start, you two."

Dinah knew she'd better talk fast.

"Guess what?"

Mrs. Seabrooke took a big bite of meat loaf and another of buttered noodles.

"I ate fourteen Dixie cups at lunch today."

Fourteen? You're kidding! That's impossible! It can't be!

"I don't remember that you cried as much as Benja-

31

min," Mrs. Seabrooke said worriedly, looking past Dinah toward Benjamin's nursery. "And I'm sure you slept more. It seems like you slept for hours and hours."

"Mom! Aren't you listening? I said, I ate fourteen Dixie cups at lunch today."

Benjamin's crying grew louder. It was more like screaming now.

"Fourteen? But why on earth— Oh, honey, I'd better go help your father. If Benjamin's hungry, he's going to keep right on crying until he's fed."

Left by herself at the table, Dinah tried one tiny, experimental sip of champagne. It tasted bitter, and the bubbles tickled the inside of her nose.

Benjamin's sobs stopped abruptly, and Mr. Seabrooke returned to his place.

"Let's eat!" he said, shaking out his napkin, but Dinah could have told him that Mrs. Kelly's wonderful meat loaf was already cold. "And weren't you going to tell me about—what was it?—a spelling contest at school?"

Not a spelling contest, an eating *contest.*

"Never mind," Dinah said.

Four

The trouble with babies, Dinah was finding out, is that they are always *there*. Dinah heard Benjamin crying every night, and awakened every morning to his insistent wail, like a dawn siren from the room next to hers. It seemed that her mother fed him all day long, and all night, too. Dinah's mother had already abandoned any hope of getting Benjamin to nurse every four hours. She claimed that Dinah, who had been a bottle-fed baby, had thrived on four-hour feedings. But the doctor had urged her to nurse Benjamin "on demand," and Benjamin made it plain that he didn't want to eat every four hours, or every three hours, or every two hours. He wanted to eat when *he* wanted to eat, and he had to be the hungriest baby in the annals of modern medicine.

When Dinah came home from school, the first thing she saw, besides the vast and spreading mess, was Benjamin eating, or sometimes, for variety, crying. If her mother had managed to coax him into napping in his little basket, as likely as not she was napping, too, leaving the house oddly quiet and still. No one had to warn Dinah now not to wake the baby. No one wanted him to sleep more than Dinah did.

She plugged him into her own version of the opening lines of "Renascence":

> All I could see from where I sat
> Was a baby big and fat;
> I turned and looked another way,
> And there that big fat baby lay.

He wasn't really fat. Dinah had just said that for the sake of the rhyme. But if he wanted to *be* fat, Dinah guessed that the way to do it was to eat ten or twelve meals a day.

Her parents were still too busy to listen to her stories, but that was okay; Dinah was too busy to tell them. With two hundred lines of poetry to memorize in two weeks, she had little time for anything else. Until "Renascence," the longest piece Dinah had ever memorized had been the Gettysburg Address. Her goal had been to recite Lincoln's words at record-breaking speed, but

"Renascence" she tried to recite slowly, with feeling. She wanted to savor every one of its four-score plus four-score plus two-score lines. Her voice filled with emotion as she practiced favorite lines: "O God, I cried, give me new birth, / And put me back upon the earth!" The rhythm and rhyme made "Renascence" easier to memorize than the Gettysburg Address had been. Once she had the first line of any couplet, the second followed inevitably in its wake. The trick was to keep all the rhyming pairs in order, and not to skip over any.

Suzanne's poem was "The Wind," by Robert Louis Stevenson. It had only eighteen lines, but Suzanne was still worried.

"What if I forget it halfway through?"

"You won't," Dinah reassured her.

"It happens to me in my piano recital every year. I get through half my piece and all of a sudden I can't remember any more, even though I played every note perfectly just the day before, and my teacher has to bring me my music in front of everyone."

"This is different. Poetry is easier. Like, the last lines of yours. How do they go?"

" 'O wind, a-blowing all day long, / O wind, that sings so loud a song!' " Suzanne recited nimbly.

"You're not going to forget those. What would you say instead? 'O wind, a-blowing all day long, / O wind, that sings so loud a tune'?"

Suzanne giggled, but she remained unconvinced. "All I know is, I want to go first and get it over with."

Going first had considerable appeal to Dinah, too, but she had decided it would be more dramatic to save hers for the very end, the climax, the grand finale.

The night before the recitation day, after Benjamin had been put to bed for as much of the night as he was going to sleep through, Dinah said "Renascence" for her parents. They sat side by side on the couch, and she stood facing them, her hands clasped loosely in front of her.

" 'All I could see from where I stood . . .' " One line followed another, smoothly, seamlessly. Dinah had been afraid her father might nod off during part of it, the way he had been doing lately in front of the evening news, but the poem apparently held him spellbound.

When she was done, when Edna St. Vincent Millay's two hundred lines had soared to their rousing conclusion, her parents pulled her down between them for a hug.

"Honey, that was simply wonderful!" her mother said, wiping tears from her eyes.

"You're a marvel," her father said. "I have trouble remembering my own Social Security number."

"Oh, Daddy." Dinah gave him a kiss. Tomorrow she would dazzle them all!

———

After lunch the next day, Mrs. Hall asked the children to clear their desks.

"We're in for a treat today," she said. "We're going to have a whole afternoon of poetry."

In response, Artie Adams fell forward over his desk, pretending that he had been stabbed in the stomach. Nathan Daniels made gagging noises.

"Unless some of you would rather spend the afternoon in Mr. Saganario's office instead."

The stabbing victim recovered promptly, and the gagging noises ceased.

"Who would like to go first?" Mrs. Hall asked. Several hands went up, including Suzanne's. But Mrs. Hall called on Mandy Bricker. Suzanne shot a despairing glance at Dinah.

Mandy took her place at the front of the classroom. "Mine's long," she said to Mrs. Hall, making it sound like an apology. "I hope that's all right."

"Oh, my, yes."

A hard lump knotted itself in the pit of Dinah's stomach.

Mandy smoothed out her skirt and adjusted the barrette that held her long dark hair back from her face.

" 'Annabel Lee,' " she said, "by Edgar Allan Poe."

The poem *was* long, and Dinah had to admit it was wonderful. How could Artie and Nathan claim not to like poetry when there were poems in the world like "Annabel Lee"? But, while Dinah had been too caught up in Mandy's recitation to count lines, she could tell the poem was shorter, much shorter, than "Renascence."

Suzanne's turn came next. Unsmiling, she got through her poem without faltering and hurried back to her seat. The general gloom that had followed Mandy's performance lifted a little bit. It was obvious that many more people had short poems, like Suzanne's, than long poems, like Mandy's.

Nathan said a funny poem by Jack Prelutsky and seemed pleased when everyone laughed. Dinah suspected that Nathan only pretended to hate poetry because Artie did.

It was hard for Dinah to relax and enjoy herself with her big moment still to come. Every time someone began a poem, her heart raced until she was sure that it was shorter than "Renascence." Even so, she wished the afternoon would never end. Poetry was so far superior to math or social studies.

Finally, only Artie and Dinah were left.

"All right, Artie, let's hear what you have for us."

Artie bounced up to Mrs. Hall's desk. "Mine is by Benjamin Franklin," he said. "Here it is:

> Haste
> Makes waste."

He was halfway back to his seat before Mrs. Hall recovered sufficiently to ask, "*That's* your poem? Three words?"

"There's probably some poem with only two," Artie said, "but I couldn't find it."

" 'Haste makes waste' isn't a *poem*, Artie. It's a"— Mrs. Hall groped for the word—"It's a maxim, a proverb."

"It rhymes," Artie pointed out. "And I found it in a poetry book. Ask Mrs. Jacob. She helped me find it."

"It would have taxed your brain too much to learn something longer?"

"No," Artie said cheerfully. "In fact, I learned another poem just in case you didn't like this one."

The teacher looked relieved. Still standing in the middle of the aisle, Artie recited:

> "Algy met a bear.
> The bear was bulgy.
> The bulge was Algy."

Then he bowed deeply and sat back down again.

Mrs. Hall joined in the laughter, but Dinah had a feeling that the mark she put next to Artie's name in her grade book wasn't a high one.

"Dinah, can you help us to end our poetry unit on a more elevated note?"

Could she? Could she ever! Dinah took her place, in the same spot where all the others had stood. She waited until she had everyone's undivided attention. After all, she had waited for this moment for two weeks already.

" 'Renascence,' by Edna St. Vincent Millay.

> All I could see from where I stood
> Was three long mountains and a wood;
> I turned and looked another way,
> And there—"

Dinah broke off mid-sentence. Something was wrong. *And there . . . And there that big fat baby lay.* That was the line from her silly Benjamin poem. The real line had three islands in it, three islands in a bay. *There lay three*

39

islands in a bay. That sounded wrong, too. And what came next? Dinah couldn't remember. Where two hundred lines of poetry had been stored in her brain, all she could find now was a great gaping hole, a hole so big and deep and wide she wished she could crawl inside it forever.

"I forgot the rest," she said in a small, strangled voice. Her poem had turned out to be three lines long, as short as Artie's.

"Do you have the poem with you?" Mrs. Hall asked sympathetically. "Do you want to read it through once more and try again?"

Dinah shook her head. This was like Suzanne's piano recitals, but a hundred times worse. Suzanne's piano recitals had happened to Suzanne. This was happening to *Dinah*.

"Why don't you go out in the hall and get a drink of water?" Mrs. Hall suggested. "Take five minutes to collect your thoughts and see if the poem doesn't come back to you."

The nicer Mrs. Hall was, the more Dinah felt like crying. It wouldn't help if she stayed by the water fountain for the rest of the year, for the rest of her life. Her moment of glory was ruined forever.

Suddenly the lost line of the poem flashed before her: *And saw three islands in a bay.* And with it, the rest of the poem floated after, like a long string of pearls.

" 'Renascence,' by Edna St. Vincent Millay," Dinah began again, before she could change her mind and flee for her seat. " 'All I could see from where I stood . . .' "

She forgot the classroom, forgot the shame of her first failed attempt. She was a nineteen-year-old poet, standing on the coast of Maine, about to lose her life and win it back again.

> "The world stands out on either side
> No wider than the heart is wide;
> Above the world is stretched the sky,—
> No higher than the soul is high.
> The heart can push the sea and land
> Farther away on either hand;
> The soul can split the sky in two,
> And let the face of God shine through.
> But East and West will pinch the heart
> That can not keep them pushed apart;
> And he whose soul is flat—the sky
> Will cave in on him by and by."

There! She was done! Spontaneously, the class burst into applause, Mrs. Hall clapping loudest of all.

"How did you do it?" Mrs. Hall asked once the commotion had subsided. "What were your tricks for memorizing such a long poem?"

Dinah hardly knew how to answer. It was like when she had first learned how to count to one hundred, years ago. For a long time it had been a major achievement to be able to count to twenty, then to thirty, to fifty. "I can count to fifty," she remembered bragging to the boy next door, only to find that he could count to sixty. But when she finally reached a hundred, it had occurred to her that if she could count to a hundred she could count to a thousand, to a million, a billion, and higher. The basic principles of counting would take her as high as she wanted to go. There was nothing left to *learn*. All she needed from that point on was time and will. All she needed was to keep on counting.

"I don't know," she said. "I just started at the beginning and kept on memorizing until I reached the end." She could memorize all the poems in the world that way, if she wanted to.

"Well, thank you," Mrs. Hall said. "That was a splendid recitation."

"You're welcome," Dinah said. Had they expected any less from Dynamite Dinah?

Five

Dinah and her mother surveyed the Seabrookes' kitchen together with dismay. Outside it was a beautiful late-March afternoon, with the first pale purple crocuses in bloom. But inside all was clutter and confusion. Dirty dishes overflowed the sink. A week's worth of unread newspapers lay in an untidy heap on the dusty tile floor. The once-gleaming counters were sticky, and the plants on the windowsill drooped for want of water.

"This," Dinah's mother said sadly, "is a poor advertisement for Seabrooke Organizing, Incorporated."

It was the week of the big spring sale at Dinah's father's store, so he had been working late every night. The day after Dinah's "Renascence" recitation, her mother had come down with a bad head cold, made worse by lack of sleep. And Benjamin—well, he was still Benjamin. Dinah had tried to help out with meals and cleaning, but her mother had run the household so efficiently in the days before Benjamin that Dinah hardly knew where to start on her own. She wasn't used to doing much more than following the step-by-step dinner instructions on her mother's weekly charts. The chart from three weeks ago still hung, forgotten, on the refrigerator door. No new charts had been posted since.

"If this were one of my client's houses, where would I tell them to begin? I used to have rules for situations like these." Mrs. Seabrooke closed her eyes to think. "Okay. Start with a relatively small job that makes a relatively big difference. What looks the worst here?"

It was hard to tell. "Everything?"

"I'd say the dishes. Why don't you load the dishwasher, and I'll take a swipe at the counters," Mrs. Seabrooke suggested.

Benjamin, who had been dozing in the baby carrier set on the kitchen table amid the morning's breakfast dishes, began to whimper.

"Better yet, why don't you entertain Benjamin, and I'll do the dishes."

That was more like it. Entertainment, after all, was Dinah's specialty.

"Benjamin! Watch me!" Dinah began curling and uncurling her tongue. Suzanne couldn't curl her tongue, however hard she tried, but Dinah could have carried off the prize at a tongue-curling championship.

Benjamin seemed to be looking, but he wasn't smiling or laughing. A whole auditorium full of babies who couldn't smile or laugh yet would drive a comedian into early retirement.

"Here, watch this, Benjamin!" Dinah made the most ferocious face she could think of. She squinched her eyes and scrunched her nose and twisted her mouth into a terrible sneer. Still no response from Benjamin.

She could try juggling. Dinah wasn't very good at juggling, but that shouldn't matter too much to Benjamin. And she'd never be any good if she didn't practice.

From the bowl on the kitchen table, Dinah took two shriveled apples and tried to toss them back and forth from one hand to the other. She missed on her first attempt, and the apples rolled across the floor.

"Dinah." Her mother sounded a warning without looking up from the sink.

"They were bruised, anyway."

Dinah tried again, and for one brief, shining moment she had both apples in the air. But in the next came catastrophe. One of the apples struck the earthenware sugar bowl at an unfortunate angle and sent it smashing from the table to the tiles below. It was easy now to answer the question, What looks the worst here? What looked the worst was the kitchen floor, littered with shards of pottery and mounds of spilled sugar.

"Dinah!"

"What goes up must come down," Dinah said lamely,

hoping her mother might see some humor in the situation. Benjamin began howling.

"Oh, Dinah." Her mother looked as if she might cry, too.

"I'll clean it up, I promise." Dinah lunged for the sponge.

"*No!* I mean, no. Just go outside and play, all right? Or go over to the Kellys'. I can't have you *and* Benjamin to worry about."

Stung by the comparison to Benjamin, the world's most useless individual, Dinah grabbed her jacket from the hook by the back door and stomped outside. She felt bad about the sugar bowl, she really did, but it had been an *accident.* Accidents could happen to anybody. And her mother had *told* her to entertain the baby.

Since Mrs. Kelly was a church organist and choir director, working irregular hours, she was home sometimes in the afternoon. And on this warm day, she was outside raking the flower beds.

"How's that beautiful baby brother of yours?" Mrs. Kelly called out as Dinah cut across the Kellys' front lawn. Snatches of Suzanne's piano exercises drifted out from the open living-room windows.

"He's okay."

Mrs. Kelly laughed. "Do I detect a lack of enthusiasm in that answer?"

"Maybe." Dinah was starting to feel better already. Mrs. Kelly always acted as if however Dinah felt about something, it was perfectly all right for her to feel that way.

Suzanne broke off practicing when Dinah came into the living room.

"I was hoping you'd come. My mom went to the store this morning, and she bought a pound-size bag of something we like."

"Does it start with an *M*?" Dinah asked.

"Yes."

Dinah knew what it was right then (she had been pretty sure before she even asked). But she and Suzanne liked to see how long they could stretch out a guessing game even when there was absolutely no suspense about the answer.

"Does it come in different colors?"

"Yes!"

"Are there two different kinds, plain and peanut?"

"Yes!"

"Does it melt in your mouth but not in your hands?"

Suzanne shook her head no.

"It doesn't?"

But Suzanne was just teasing. "Of course it does. They're in the kitchen. Come on."

The Kellys' kitchen was so big it had a real working fireplace in it, like in pioneer days. The family ate most of their meals in the kitchen, on the stout oaken trestle table, with its long cushioned benches on each side. Mrs. Kelly's collection of antique cookie cutters decorated the walls, and a great jumble of battered copper pots hung from the rafters. It was Dinah's favorite spot on earth, especially when there was a pound bag of M&M's hidden in a crockery jar on top of the refrigerator.

47

Suzanne climbed up to get it. "I put it up high so I wouldn't eat them all before you got here."

She and Dinah began counting the candies into two small bowls—the red, orange, and yellow ones for Dinah, green and the two shades of brown for Suzanne. The color sorting was an ancient ritual, dating back to the earliest days of their friendship, in third grade, when Dinah's family had just moved to their house on the corner of Barclay Avenue and Tulip Street. Dinah wasn't Dynamite Dinah yet, but she had liked to give herself grand-sounding names like the kings and queens in library books: Dinah the Lionhearted, Dinah the Conqueror.

"You need a name, too," she had told Suzanne on the first day they played together after school. "Suzanne the Brave? Suzanne the Great?" Neither name had seemed particularly apt, but they had been the best Dinah could come up with.

"I'm not all that brave," Suzanne had said, always honest. "Or great, either."

"What are you?"

"I don't know. I try to be nice, I guess."

Soon Dinah the Conqueror was paying daily visits to Suzanne the Nice. And in the Kellys' big kitchen they would eat M&M's, sorting them into two paper cups, so each could have the colors she liked, even if in fact all the colors tasted the same.

Mrs. Kelly came in from gardening as the last of the M&M's were shaken from the bag, Tom behind her.

"You don't have to eat them *all* today, girls," she said.

"When I bought that bag this morning, I hoped it would last you the week. Suzanne, love, put half of those away for later. Dinah can take the rest of hers home with her when she goes."

"*If* I go," Dinah said.

"Uh-oh," Tom said.

"My mom's in kind of a bad mood," Dinah explained. She launched into the story of the Unappreciated Juggler.

"So I picked up two apples, like this?" Dinah stood up and took two shiny red apples from the basket on the trestle table. It was considerate of people to keep their kitchens well stocked with juggling materials. "And I was going to show Benjamin how to juggle. But the trouble is, I can't juggle very well. But how am I ever going to learn if I don't practice?"

"Of course," Tom said.

"So I tried tossing them up in the air, you know, one in each hand?"

"Show us," Tom suggested wickedly.

"Maybe outside," Mrs. Kelly began, but it was too late. Without thinking, Dinah had flung both apples up in the air. One landed harmlessly on the floor, but the other would have struck the now-empty M&M's jar if Tom hadn't caught it in the nick of time. If only Tom had been so conveniently situated an hour ago.

"So that's what happened. Only Tom wasn't there to catch it. So it hit the sugar bowl instead." Dinah sat down, her story done.

"But didn't it break?" Suzanne asked. "The sugar bowl, I mean."

"Oh, it broke, all right. It was smashed to smithereens." *Smithereens.* Now, there was a wonderful word.

"I think I'm beginning to understand your mother's 'bad mood,' " Mrs. Kelly said. "Dinah, Dinah, Dinah. Your family's in for some changes, and you're going to have to be part of them. You're going to have to think before you juggle."

That was all she said, but Dinah felt a pang of guilt. She could tell that Mrs. Kelly didn't think the juggling story was as funny as she had meant it to be.

"I guess Benjamin's turning out to be a lot of work for my mom." After all, the broken sugar bowl really was as much Benjamin's fault as Dinah's. Or almost as much. Or a little bit his fault, at least.

"I remember what a friend told me when I had my second child," Mrs. Kelly said. "She told me: One is like one, two is like ten."

"What's four like?" Tom asked.

"I can't count that high." Mrs. Kelly grinned at him. "Listen, Dinah, I have a pan of lasagna in the deep freeze, and I'm going to send it home with you. I have a feeling your mother could do without cooking tonight."

When Dinah reached home, the dishes were done and the floor was swept; but she could still feel some gritty grains of sugar crunching underfoot when she walked over to set the pan down on the counter.

"Look what Mrs. Kelly sent," Dinah said, hoping one pan of lasagna would cancel out one sugar bowl.

Her mother looked up from nursing Benjamin. "Lasagna? I mean it, what would we do without Jane?"

Dinah picked up the last stray piece of broken sugar bowl from the floor by the sink. "And, Mom? I'm sorry about the sugar bowl. And I'm going to help more around the house. I really am."

Mrs. Seabrooke shifted Benjamin to the other side and with her free hand pulled Dinah close for a hug.

"It's been a rough few weeks," she admitted. "I don't know how other people do it. I mean, at least I'm organized. Think what it would be like around here if I wasn't."

True to her word, after school the next day, Dinah volunteered to take Benjamin out for a ride in his stroller.

"That would be a big help," her mother said, eyeing the overflowing laundry basket. "I could certainly use an hour without Master Benjamin. But, Dinah, no circus stunts. Don't try to push the stroller backward while balancing a banana on the end of your nose, okay?"

"Mom!" Really, where did grown-ups get such strange ideas?

The Seabrookes lived on a hilly street, so steep that children from blocks around used it for sledding on snowy days. But the last snow had melted weeks before, and Dinah gulped down big breaths of balmy spring air as she pushed Benjamin's stroller up sidewalks lined with daffodils. The stroller was heavy, and Dinah was panting by the time she reached the small park at the top of the hill.

Dinah peeked at Benjamin. He was sound asleep. Carefully, she turned the stroller so the sun wouldn't be in his eyes and set the brake so he wouldn't roll away.

Then she settled herself on one of the swings and scuffed her shoes back and forth in the sandy dirt.

I sit on a swing / Glad that it's spring. Another first line. As she swung and scuffed, scuffed and swung, Dinah chewed on a long piece of onion grass that she had stopped to pick on the way. She felt happier than she had for a long time, since her rain dance on the day Benjamin was born.

It wasn't so bad being a big sister. Sleeping beneath his crocheted blanket, Benjamin looked so sweet, so small and soft and trusting. A quick half-smile passed across his face, like a thin ray of shifting sunlight. The nurse in the hospital had told Dinah that when a newborn baby smiled like that, it meant either that he had gas or that he was dreaming of angels.

Would Dinah send Benjamin away if she could? The other day, when he had cried through dinner and spoiled every single one of Dinah's stories, she had imagined leaving him, in his basket, by the side of the road for some other family to find. She'd pack up all his little clothes to go with him—the terry-cloth stretchies and the tiny nightgowns and the soft yellow bunting with Paddington Bear on it. Good-bye, Benjamin! Pinned to his blanket she'd leave a note, so that passersby would understand that his parents and sister didn't need him back anytime soon: "Please take me home with you. My family doesn't want me because I cry too much, but I'm really a very nice baby. Yours truly, Benjamin Seabrooke." But the note was too sad to write. Dinah had been ready to cry just thinking about it. And all those little outfits, freshly washed and neatly folded . . .

Dinah had wanted a baby brother all her life, and now she had one, even if so far he wasn't working out the way anyone had planned. "You can stay, Benjamin," Dinah said out loud, from the swing. Benjamin stirred in his sleep, so Dinah said it again more softly. "You can stay."

Six

_____

T he first week in April, Mrs. Hall announced that Room 5A's spring play would be *The Adventures of Tom Sawyer*. She handed out mimeographed copies of the play so that students could read it before the auditions on Friday.

Dinah fought back disappointment. The best parts in *The Adventures of Tom Sawyer* were for boys—Tom Sawyer and Huckleberry Finn. But when she read through the play (secretly, during social studies), she decided that she wouldn't mind playing Becky Thatcher or Aunt Polly. Aunt Polly would be the more challenging of the two roles. Dinah would have to use all her acting skill to portray the spinster aunt who scolds Tom mercilessly for his pranks but deep down loves him with all her heart. But Becky was in more scenes, with twice as many lines to speak. And it would be fun to play Tom Sawyer's sweetheart, especially in the most exciting scene of the play, when the two children are lost in the cave, facing death together.

"Who do you think she'll pick for Tom?" Dinah asked Suzanne as they lay on Suzanne's bed after school, eating bits and pieces of the big chocolate rabbit left over from Suzanne's Easter basket. Tom and Becky held hands in the cave scene, so it mattered a lot to Dinah which boy played Tom.

"Artie would make the best Tom, don't you think?"

Dinah agreed. Besides, although she wouldn't have admitted it, even to Suzanne, she liked Artie best of all the boys.

"Tom has a lot of lines to speak," Dinah pointed out. She took a bite out of one chocolate rabbit's ear. "And you remember how short Artie's poem was."

"He's just lazy. He could learn Tom's lines if he wanted to."

"Will Mrs. Hall think so?"

Suzanne nibbled on the rabbit's other ear. "I guess it depends on how he acts during the auditions."

"If I'm Becky, who will be Aunt Polly?"

"Mandy. You both got the two best girl's parts in the other plays."

The fall play had been *Caddie Woodlawn*. Mandy had been Caddie, which Dinah admitted had to count as the starring role. But it had been Dinah's portrayal of Caddie's prissy, stuck-up Cousin Annabelle that had made the audience roar with laughter. To Annabelle had belonged the funniest scene in the play, the one where the others slip a raw egg down the back of her dress as she's about to turn a somersault. Annabelle's cry of bewildered dismay, "This—this—*this* is *squishy!*" had brought down the house.

The winter play had been the story of a girl who, in a dream, travels to various magical kingdoms, sort of like *The Nutcracker*, without any music or dancing and without the nutcracker. Dinah had been the girl, the only person onstage during every single scene of the play. Other people's parents had kept coming up to her afterward, telling her, "You should be an actress, young lady!" Which was exactly what Dinah planned to be.

"Do you think I should be Becky Thatcher or Aunt Polly?" Dinah asked her parents at dinner that night. They were having take-out Chinese food, left over from the night before. Benjamin was dozing in his windup swing, so Dinah had her parents' full attention.

"If you ask me, you bring Tom to mind more than Becky or Polly," Mr. Seabrooke said. "Maybe Mrs. Hall would be willing to rewrite the play a little bit and call it *The Adventures of Tomasina.*"

Dinah was pleased, but she knew it would never happen. "She'd have to rewrite it a *lot*, to make Tom a girl."

"You know we'll come, whichever part you play," Mrs. Seabrooke said. "Or your father will. I don't think Benjamin is ready yet for an afternoon at the theater."

"You could get a baby-sitter." For all Dinah knew,

there might not be plays next year, in sixth grade. This might be her mother's last chance for a long time to see Dinah in a starring role.

"We'll see," her mother said. "I can't really leave Benjamin for more than two hours because of the nursing. You know how he screams if I try to give him a bottle. But we'll probably be able to work something out."

"Maybe we'd better get your autograph now, before you get too famous," Dinah's father joked.

Benjamin woke up halfway through dessert. Always the first to finish, Dinah took him on her lap.

"Hi, Benjamin! It's me, Dinah!"

Benjamin didn't smile, but he didn't cry, either. Dinah's parents claimed that Benjamin cried less when Dinah held him. So far, not crying was the most anybody could hope for from Benjamin. If Benjamin wasn't crying, the family interpreted it as meaning that he liked something. In this way the Seabrookes had decided that Benjamin liked music, his bath, car rides, stroller rides, and Dinah.

"See, we told you he likes you," Mrs. Seabrooke said, as Benjamin stared up intently into Dinah's face.

Dinah gave the baby her pinkie finger to hold and his tiny fist curled around it. "Do you think I should be Aunt Polly or Becky Thatcher?" she asked him. Benjamin kept on staring.

Actually, though she didn't want to say anything about it to her parents, Dinah was beginning to worry about Benjamin. She had known, of course, that he wouldn't walk or talk at first, wouldn't even sit up or roll over. But he was almost five weeks old now, and his accomplishments were still so few. He could eat and sleep and cry and burp and pee and poop and spit up. He could look at things. He could grasp somebody's finger. And he could hold his head up.

This last seemed to impress visitors. "Look how well he holds his head up!" they'd say. Dinah's parents would beam, but such compliments made Dinah feel sad for Benjamin. If that was all you could be complimented for, it would be better not to get any compliments at all.

———

Mrs. Hall always conducted auditions in the same way. After lunch, the students cleared their desks except for their copies of the play. Mrs. Hall wrote the list of all the characters in the play on the chalkboard, in two columns, one for boys and one for girls. Next to each character's name she wrote the names of the students who wanted to try out for that part. Then all the students who wanted to play, for example, Tom and Becky would take turns coming to the front of the room and reading a scene with Tom and Becky in it.

It made for a long afternoon, since some scenes were read over and over again with different readers each time. But Dinah found it fascinating to hear the same lines spoken in so many different ways. And seldom did anyone read a part better than she did. At least that's what Dinah thought, trying to listen impartially.

This time every girl in the class wanted to play Becky.

Dinah put up her hand to read for Becky and for Aunt Polly, too. The boys were more divided, with some preferring Tom, some preferring Huck, and some determined to escape any speaking part at all. Artie was reading for both Tom and Huck. Evidently, on this occasion he was willing to memorize something longer than "Algy met a bear" or "Haste makes waste."

Dinah was the third girl to read for Becky, reading opposite Artie, as Tom. She read so well that she knew the part was all but hers. Artie did well, too, his eyes full of mischief, a swagger in his step. He would definitely get the part of Tom, if there was any justice in the world.

The only way Dinah could fail to be Becky would be if Mrs. Hall decided she simply had to save Dinah to play Aunt Polly. Although several girls would make passable Beckys, including Mandy Bricker and even Suzanne, Dinah had to admit that none of the others came close to her reading of Aunt Polly. Joan Whiting had read Aunt Polly's lines with lively expression, but Joan was short and chubby, completely wrong for Dinah's mental picture of Tom's sharp-tongued aunt. So maybe Dinah would have to play Aunt Polly, by default. But it seemed unfair that Dinah should get the second-best girl's part just because she was a *better* actress than the girls trying out for the best part.

Finally everybody had read, though why some kids had bothered to try out Dinah didn't know. If you knew you weren't good enough to be cast, why drag out the auditions? Like Suzanne, for example. The other day

Suzanne had come right out and said that the two best parts would go to Dinah and Mandy. Yet when Mrs. Hall had asked who wanted to play Becky, Suzanne had raised her hand along with everybody else.

For the other two plays, Mrs. Hall had read her cast list right away, that same afternoon. After all, in most cases the choices were obvious. Dinah had looked forward to having the whole weekend to begin learning her lines, whether Becky's or Polly's. But this time Mrs. Hall dismissed class for the day without announcing any casting decisions.

"You all read wonderfully," she said. "I'll have the cast list ready for you on Monday."

Dinah couldn't possibly wait till then.

"But, Mrs. Hall . . ." she called out, without raising her hand.

"On Monday," Mrs. Hall repeated. So that was that.

Dinah had never lived through a longer weekend. To pass the time, she went to the mall with Suzanne on Saturday, even though she hated shopping. On Sunday, Dinah took Benjamin for another stroller ride, the first since the sugar-bowl episode. She kept meaning to help her mother more after school, but forgetting to offer until Benjamin was already in bed for the night. And this stroller ride didn't make Dinah want to volunteer for another tour of duty anytime soon. Benjamin howled the whole way to the park and back again.

———

"What if Mrs. Hall doesn't read the list until three

o'clock?" Dinah asked Suzanne as they walked to school together on Monday morning.

Suzanne, who had nothing to worry about, shrugged. "Then I guess we'll have to wait until three."

But after the flag salute, Mrs. Hall gave the class a smile. "I know you're all anxious to hear the cast list for *The Adventures of Tom Sawyer*. I had some hard decisions to make, but I think I've put together a strong cast."

Hard decisions. That had to mean that Dinah would be playing Aunt Polly and not Becky Thatcher. Oh, but she would have done such a spectacular job as Becky in the cave scene!

"The cast, in order of appearance: Tom Sawyer, Artie Adams. Aunt Polly, Joan Whiting." Dinah went limp with relief. She would be Becky, after all. "Huckleberry Finn, Nathan Daniels. Becky Thatcher, Suzanne Kelly. Injun Joe, Douglas DeSoto . . ."

Dinah couldn't believe it. Mrs. Hall must have read the list wrong. *Suzanne* as Becky Thatcher? Suzanne couldn't act. Joan Whiting as Aunt Polly and *Suzanne* as Becky Thatcher? The play was ruined right there. It would be so bad it would be embarrassing. All the members of Room 5A would have to wear bags over their heads for the rest of their lives.

There had to be a mistake. Dinah looked over at Suzanne. Suzanne was blushing with pleasure, and right then Dinah hated her. How dare Suzanne think she had a right to play Becky Thatcher? If Suzanne were truly

Dinah's best friend, she would march right up to Mrs. Hall's desk and say, "Thank you, but I don't deserve to play Becky. Dinah read the best on Friday, and the part should go to her." But Suzanne sat there with a ridiculous smile plastered across her face.

Mrs. Hall kept on reading. "Village Girls One, Two, and Three, Mandy Bricker, Dinah Seabrooke, and Eileen McDonald . . ."

So Dinah was going to have a one-line part. Her whole part was to say one line in the classroom scene, and then to wave a flag in the big crowd scene at the end of the play, when Tom and Becky (Artie and *Suzanne*) were rescued from the cave and welcomed home again. Village Girl Number Two was worse than no part at all. Mrs. Hall had added insult to injury.

Dinah wasn't going to cry. Not if she died from the pain. She tried to smile as if Village Girl Number Two was the part she had really wanted, anyway. She couldn't make her mouth form itself into a smiling shape. But she didn't cry.

All morning long, Dinah didn't cry, through math and spelling and art. At last, the bell rang for lunch.

Dinah wanted to sweep out of the classroom and down to the cafeteria without a word or gesture that would betray what she was feeling. But anger was stronger in her than pride. Someone had to confront Mrs. Hall with the terrible truth of her unfairness. It was properly Suzanne's job, or Joan's. Apparently they didn't care whether they deserved their roles or not. But if they wouldn't speak up against the injustice, Dinah would.

She waited until the rest of the class had filed out of the room. Then she made her way to the teacher's desk.

"Mrs. Hall?" Dinah struggled to speak over the enormous lump in her throat. "Why did—you know I read better than Suzanne or Joan. Why did you pick them and not me?"

"Oh, Dinah," Mrs. Hall said. She looked troubled. "I was hoping you wouldn't take it so hard. I know you're the most talented actress in the class. But you've had your turn at a major role twice now. This isn't Broadway, where my only concern would be to mount a Tony-Award-winning production. I have to try to be fair to everyone. Suzanne and Joan deserve some time in the spotlight, too."

"Not if they're not the best for the part. They'll ruin the play for everyone."

"Now, Dinah, let's not exaggerate. I think you'll be surprised at what a good job they'll do. And look at it from their point of view. How would you like to be always on the sidelines, always passed over in favor of the one or two stars?"

"I wouldn't mind, not if the stars were really better than I was."

"You would, Dinah. Believe me. Everyone wants to be a star, Suzanne and Joan as much as you."

It began to sink in: Mrs. Hall wasn't going to change her mind. She had as much as admitted that Dinah deserved the role that had gone to Suzanne, but she wasn't going to do anything about it.

"Try to understand, okay, Dinah? Don't begrudge Suzanne her day in the sun."

"Okay," Dinah managed to say. "Can I go now?"

Mrs. Hall nodded. But instead of joining the others in the cafeteria, Dinah fled down the hall in the opposite direction, to the girls' lavatory by the first- and second-grade rooms. No big kids would find her there. And then she locked herself inside one of the tiny cubicles and cried as if her heart would break.

Seven

When Dinah was seven, she had gotten a bad case of chicken pox. She still remembered sleepless nights, her hands wrapped in gauze bandages to keep her from scratching those itching, burning sores. Nothing, she had thought at the time, could ever hurt more than chicken pox.

Now she knew better. Worse than chicken pox was to sit and watch your best friend rehearsing the part you had wanted, but didn't get. Mrs. Hall held rehearsals for *Tom Sawyer* every day from two to three. For Dinah, that hour was a black hole of misery.

The first rehearsal was on the same day the cast list

65

was announced. It was a "read through" rehearsal—people read their lines from their seats rather than acting the parts in front of the room. Dinah's one line didn't come up until halfway through the play. But she followed along with her script, anyway, still unable to let go of a desperate half-hope that somehow, in a miraculously altered version of the play, Tom's sweetheart, the girl who gets lost with him in the cave, wasn't Becky Thatcher at all, but Village Girl Number Two.

"It's ever so nice—I wish I could draw," Suzanne-as-Becky read.

Dinah put her head down on her desk, behind the barricade of her folded arms.

"Dinah?" Mrs. Hall asked. "Do you feel all right?"

"Not really," Dinah said. Maybe Mrs. Hall would send her to the nurse and she'd miss the rest of that day's rehearsal. "I think I'm going to throw up."

That made for a stir in the classroom, as those in the desks nearest to Dinah looked over at her with horrified fascination. But Dinah was almost too wretched to care. The more she thought about it, the more she *did* feel sick to her stomach.

"Try taking a few deep breaths and see if that helps," Mrs. Hall said, obviously unconvinced. Dinah wished she could throw up on the spot just to show her.

At a sign from Mrs. Hall, Suzanne resumed reading. Escape to the nurse's office was becoming increasingly urgent.

"Mrs. Hall!" Dinah held her stomach and moaned.

Mrs. Hall sighed. "All right, Dinah, you can go see Mrs. Riley. But if there's nothing wrong with you, I want you back here in ten minutes."

Really! If only Mrs. Riley would discover that Dinah had a terrible stomach disease. Mrs. Hall would feel guilty for years for having doubted her. *How could I have thought she was faking when she really had leprosy of the stomach?*

But Mrs. Riley didn't even take Dinah's temperature before sending her back to class. "You're right as rain," she said cheerfully. As if you could tell whether a person had stomach leprosy just by *looking*. But at least the rehearsal was almost over by the time Dinah returned.

At the closing bell, Dinah darted out the classroom door. She was halfway down the hall before she heard Suzanne calling after her, "Dinah! Wait up!"

Dinah hesitated. To be fair, it wasn't really Suzanne's fault that she had been cast as Becky. Reluctantly, Dinah let Suzanne fall into step beside her.

"Where were you at lunch?" Suzanne asked. "Was your stomach bothering you then, too?"

"Kind of."

"Mrs. Hall's awful. You'd have to practically die on the floor in front of her for her to think you were sick."

Suzanne's loyalty in siding with Dinah against Mrs. Hall made the knot of pain in Dinah's abdomen ease a little bit. If Suzanne would apologize for getting Dinah's part, Dinah might try to forgive her for taking it.

"Oh, congratulations," Dinah said, trying to sound

breezy and offhand. "On being Becky." There, she had said it. Now Suzanne could say, *But you were the one who deserved it.*

"Thanks," Suzanne said.

Thanks?

"But—" Suzanne began, and then broke off. Dinah looked at her expectantly. "I mean, are you sure you don't mind? Because I know how much you wanted to play Becky."

Not *wanted* to, *deserved* to. The difference was crucial. Dinah couldn't bear the thought that Suzanne might be feeling not outrage on her behalf, but pity.

"No, I didn't," Dinah said quickly. "I thought I might want to play Aunt Polly, but I'm just as glad I didn't get it. I'm getting pretty tired of acting."

If Suzanne saw through this—even Dinah was embarrassed at the transparency of the lie—she didn't let on.

"Well, you were in both other plays. And you're *in* this one, too."

"That's right," Dinah said. "I have a great part. I'm Village Girl Number Two!"

She waited for Suzanne to burst out laughing. If it weren't so tragic that Dinah had a one-line part, it could be viewed as rather funny. Hilarious even. Dinah, who had played Cousin Annabelle and starred in the Christmas play—Dinah, who should have played Becky Thatcher, Aunt Polly, or even, in her father's view, Tomasina—Dinah, the best actress in the class—*Dinah*, cast as Village Girl Number Two?

But Suzanne said seriously, "Some kids didn't get *any* part."

Did Suzanne think Dinah should be *grateful* to be Village Girl Number Two? That Suzanne's perception of the casting could be that radically different from her own made Dinah feel like Alice, tumbling down the rabbit hole into a topsy-turvy Wonderland.

As if sensing that she had said something wrong, Suzanne changed the subject. "Let's go to your house today. We can play with Benjamin."

"Okay," Dinah said, glad to let the subject drop. It would be a relief if she never had to talk about *The Adventures of Tom Sawyer* again.

Suzanne adored babies. When she visited the Seabrookes, she pounced on Benjamin and made him her baby for the afternoon. Dinah didn't mind changing Benjamin's diaper if her parents were busy, but Suzanne viewed any chance to diaper Benjamin as a special treat. You'd think Suzanne was Benjamin's mother herself, the way she bustled back and forth importantly with him in her arms.

"You are *so* lucky," she'd say to Dinah, as she held Benjamin's pacifier in his little mouth. It was a shame, in a way, that Dinah and Suzanne couldn't trade brothers, Benjamin in exchange for Tom.

Now Suzanne reached for Benjamin, lying in Dinah's mother's arms, before she had even taken off her jacket. Mrs. Seabrooke grinned and let her take him.

"How was school today, girls?" Dinah dreaded the

question that was going to come next. If only she hadn't talked about the play before the casting. "And the play! So which is it? Becky Thatcher or Aunt Polly?"

"Neither!" Dinah said brightly. "Suzanne is going to be Becky, and Joan Whiting is going to be Aunt Polly. I'm Village Girl Number Two!"

"Why, Suzanne! Congratulations!" Dinah's mother did a good job of hiding her surprise, but she gave Dinah's hand an extra squeeze. "I'll go fix us all a snack to celebrate."

Mrs. Seabrooke returned with three wine glasses, filled to the brim with sparkling ginger ale. "We can pretend it's champagne," she said, and raised her glass for a toast. "To my two favorite actresses."

Dinah drank a sip of hers and put her glass back on the tray. "I don't feel very good," she said. "My stomach hurts. It hurts a lot."

"Poor darling," her mother said. "When did it start hurting?"

"I don't remember," Dinah said, but of course she remembered very well.

She suspected that her mother knew, too. But she let her mother help her into her pajamas and tuck her into bed. Lying there under the covers, she could hear the rise and fall of voices, her mother and Suzanne still talking in the kitchen. Suzanne liked Dinah's mother the same way Dinah liked Suzanne's.

When Dinah woke up a couple of hours later, Suzanne had gone. The afternoon sun was fading against the wallpaper, and her mother had brought her supper on a tray. Mrs. Seabrooke knew exactly what to do for stomachaches like Dinah's.

During the next day's rehearsal, Dinah drew an elaborate pattern of red pockmarks on her left arm with a red pen.

"Mrs. Hall!" she blurted out as Artie and Suzanne were going through their lines for the cave scene. "Can I go to the nurse? I have a terrible rash all over my arm."

Mrs. Hall came over to look.

"I wouldn't get too close," Dinah advised. "You might catch it."

"I certainly hope what you have isn't catching," Mrs. Hall snapped. She took away Dinah's red pen. "One more peep out of you, Dinah, and you can spend the rest of the rehearsal in Mr. Saganario's office.

Mrs. Hall should have known better.

"Peep," Dinah said.

"Okay, Dinah, that does it. Out you go!"

On Wednesday Dinah decided against developing the hacking cough she had planned. Mrs. Hall might take away her one poor, pathetic line if she kept interrupting the rehearsals. Much as she sneered at Village Girl Number Two, it would be worse to be cut off from the play altogether. She tried to listen objectively during the rehearsal that day to see if Suzanne and Joan were doing as badly as she had predicted they would. Joan was doing surprisingly well as Aunt Polly, but Dinah couldn't hear Suzanne saying Becky's lines without imagining how much better they could be said by somebody else.

"How do you think it's going?" Suzanne asked her afterward. They were at Suzanne's, playing back the episode of "General Hospital" Suzanne had taped on her family's VCR.

"It's fine," Dinah said, trying to act absorbed in the on-screen love scene between a male and a female surgeon.

"Do you really think so?"

Dinah hated it when people fished for compliments. "I *said* so."

"Isn't Artie wonderful as Tom?"

Dinah shrugged. She didn't think anything about the play was wonderful, if Suzanne wanted to know the truth.

"At least he's memorizing more than three lines this time," Dinah said. "Speaking of which—I wonder if Mrs. Hall will have us memorize any more poems this year. It would be fun if we memorized poems again and Mrs. Hall had the parents in to hear us recite them. Or we could give an assembly of poems for the whole school."

"It's enough for me just memorizing Becky's lines. Becky has a *lot* of lines, and I'm not good at memorizing like you are. I had a dream last night that it was the play, and I opened my mouth to say Becky's first line and nothing came out. I just about died."

"I might start memorizing another real long poem, just in case," Dinah said, refusing to offer Suzanne any reassurance. "Mrs. Jacob said 'Casey at the Bat' is long, but it sounds like it's about baseball or something. I don't want to do a poem about baseball."

"Of course, someone will be in the wings to prompt me if I do forget anything. Like in the cave scene, where I have the most lines. Did you think I was overacting today in the cave scene? Artie gave me a look during it, like: Enough is enough already! But, I mean, if Becky really thinks she's *dying*—"

"Maybe Edna St. Vincent Millay wrote other poems. Other long ones."

Suzanne clicked off the TV. "You're not even listening," she said flatly.

"I am, too."

"What did I just say?"

"Something about the play." Dinah stopped, and then the words came in a rush. "Isn't that all you can talk about? Play, play, play. And you weren't listening to me, either."

"But I was talking first. You interrupted."

"It's not interrupting to change the subject after one person's been going on and on about something. There's more than one topic in the universe, you know."

"*You* only have one topic," Suzanne said under her breath.

"What?" Dinah had a different batch of stories every day.

"Yourself."

Dinah stared at Suzanne. She didn't think her friend had it in her to say something that would hurt so deeply.

73

Suzanne made it sound as if Dinah were a bad person, selfish and self-centered. But why shouldn't Dinah talk about herself sometimes? Suzanne would have to admit that, for all her faults, Dinah was at least *interesting*.

"Do you know what Mrs. Hall told me?" Dinah asked. "She said she just gave you the part of Becky because she felt sorry for you. *Poor* Suzanne, who never gets anything. And you do overact in the cave scene. You can't act, and you know it."

Dinah could hardly believe she was talking like this to her best friend.

"Maybe you'd better go," Suzanne said.

"Oh, I'm going, all right."

Suzanne clicked the TV back on, just the picture without the sound. Dinah picked up her backpack and her jacket and her hat, and walked out the door without looking back.

Eight

Dinah waited for almost ten minutes at the corner of Suzanne's street, to give Suzanne time to come after her. Even when she finally made herself start toward home, she walked in slow motion, her ears straining for the sound of Suzanne's footsteps behind her. *Dinah, come back! I didn't mean what I said. Honest, I didn't.* And then she could tell Suzanne that she hadn't meant what she said, either, and they could be friends again.

The phone rang after dinner.

"I'll get it!" Dinah yelled.

But when she grabbed the receiver, it wasn't Suzanne at all, but a man from a carpet-cleaning service. Eight-thirty, and Suzanne still hadn't called. Dinah's bedtime was at nine. How could she go to bed, how could she sleep, with Suzanne's accusation hammering in her ears: *You have only one topic: yourself.* And her own reply: *Mrs. Hall just gave you the part because she felt sorry for you.* Cruel, spiteful words, hurled at Suzanne to hurt her as deeply as she had hurt Dinah.

Nine o'clock. Should Dinah call Suzanne? What could she say? *I'm sorry.* But Dinah wasn't sorry unless Suzanne was sorry, too, unless Suzanne was sorry first.

"Bedtime for you, pumpkin," Dinah's father said.

"But— Well, can I stay up? Just this once? I'm expecting an important phone call."

"From? Do you want to fill us in on something?"

Dinah shook her head.

"Come on, honey, off to bed. We'll get you up if they call to say you've won the Publishers Clearing House Sweepstakes."

Even in bed, Dinah lay awake for a long, long time, willing the phone to ring. *Mr. Seabrooke, I'm sorry to be calling so late, but I have to talk to Dinah.* In almost three years of friendship, she and Suzanne had never had a fight. But if Suzanne thought Dinah talked only about herself, if she thought Dinah was vain and self-centered, then how could she have been Dinah's friend for so long?

Sunlight slanted through Dinah's windows. It was morning, and Suzanne hadn't called. Dinah knew then that Suzanne would never call. Which was worse, losing the part of Becky to your best friend or losing your best friend altogether? But if that was how Suzanne wanted it, that was how Dinah wanted it, too.

When Dinah saw Suzanne that morning on the blacktop outside school, for a moment it seemed that Suzanne was looking at her searchingly, expecting her to say something. Dinah gave her an icy stare and went over to talk to Mandy. Later, out of the corner of her eye, she saw that Suzanne was talking to Joan Whiting.

Dinah's friendship with Suzanne was over, over forever.

———

By the middle of April everyone agreed: Benjamin was smiling. Dinah had thought that a baby's first smile would be as obvious as a jack-o'-lantern's grin. One moment all you have is a pumpkin with two eyes and a nose carved on one side; then you carve in a row of jagged teeth, and ta-dah! The pumpkin smiles. Benjamin's first smile wasn't like that. From the start, fleeting smiles would flit across his face, but Dinah knew those were only gas or dreaming-of-angels smiles. Benjamin couldn't yet smile *at* anybody. But after a while, sometimes Benjamin's mouth would seem to give an upward twist if you leaned over his basket and talked to him. "There! Is *that* a smile?" one of the Seabrookes would ask. But before the others could gather for an opinion, Benjamin's expression would have changed again.

Now, however, no one needed to ask, "Is *that* a

smile?" Of course it was! Gradually, not-quite-smiles had turned into great big smiles, like the jack-o'-lantern's, but without any teeth.

Dinah was thrilled.

"Here, Benjamin, smile!" She would give him her own biggest smile, and, sure enough, he would smile back. It made Dinah want to snatch Benjamin out of his baby carrier and cover him with kisses. Dinah's parents apparently felt the same way. They spent hours coaxing smiles out of Benjamin. It was odd to see big, tall grownups trying so hard to please one small baby. What a strange world it was! After all, smiling was a bit like holding your head up. All normal people could do it. Why make such a big fuss over one toothless grin? But everyone did, Dinah, too.

Suzanne would have been in ecstasy over Benjamin's new smiling ability, but she hadn't seen one of his full-fledged smiles yet. It had been a week since the girls had quarreled, and they still weren't speaking. Dinah had taken to having lunch with Mandy and her friends: Village girls had to stick together. Although she pretended not to notice, she saw that Suzanne was spending more time with Joan. Fine! They could dwell on every detail about *Tom Sawyer* to their hearts' content, until even they got sick of the sound of their own voices.

But after school each day, walking home alone with the pain of the play rehearsal still smarting, Dinah's proud sore heart ached inside her. She definitely missed Suzanne, the old Suzanne, Suzanne the Nice. She missed Suzanne's family—Mrs. Kelly, who understood Dinah's feelings so well, Mr. Kelly, always calm and smiling, and Tom. Just because she was no longer friends with Suzanne, did she have to give up her friendship with the rest of the Kellys as well? That didn't seem fair.

Dinah knew that her parents missed Suzanne, too. She had tried to evade their questions about the quarrel, but they kept on asking. Dinah could tell that, however much they loved their own daughter, they had trouble believing that a fight between Dinah and Suzanne could possibly be Suzanne's fault.

Finally, on the Tuesday afternoon before the play, when she knew Suzanne would be at her piano lesson, Dinah walked over to the Kellys' big, sprawling blue house on Spruce Street. There was no harm in just walking by; Dinah had as much right to use the sidewalk as anybody else.

As she had hoped, Tom was in the driveway, taking practice lay-up shots at the basketball hoop hung over the garage door. Dinah pretended not to see him. Looking neither to the left nor to the right, she strode along briskly.

"Dynamite!" Tom dribbled the ball in place as he called after her. "Can't you say hello?"

Dinah stopped walking. "Hello," she said, relieved that Tom at least was still speaking to her.

"Or, how about: hello, how are you?"

"Hello, how are you?"

"*I'm* fine." He tossed her the basketball, and Dinah managed to catch it. "It's you I'm worried about. What's with you and Suzy?"

Hugging the ball to her chest, Dinah edged over to where Tom was standing. "We had a fight."

"No kidding. Do you want to talk about it?"

Haltingly, Dinah told him the story, wondering if Tom would side with her against his own sister. But the Kellys never took sides. Or, rather, they seemed to be on everybody's side.

"So, basically, you're jealous of Suzy." Dinah started to protest, but Tom held up his hand. "Who wouldn't be, under the circumstances? And it's rough being Town Girl Number Two."

"Village Girl," Dinah corrected.

"But you know what? Suzy's really blossoming. If it weren't for this dumb fight with you, she'd be walking on air. I've heard her practicing her lines, and, if you'll forgive me for saying so, I think she makes a terrific Becky. Face it, Dynamite, Suzy's more the Becky type. You're more of a Tom, female version, of course."

"That's what my father says."

Tom took the ball from Dinah and tossed it in the direction of the basket. It struck the backboard, then dropped through the hoop with a satisfying *swish*.

"There's a saying that goes something like this: 'There are no small parts, only small players.' Do you know what that means?"

Dinah shook her head.

"Even the smallest part can be played to perfection. You can have one line, but say it so well that the audience is still thinking about that one line when they leave the theater. Sometimes a person with a tiny walk-on part ends up stealing the show, because she makes the short time she's onstage so memorable. In a way, it's up to you how good a part Village Girl Number Two turns out to be."

Something like hope fluttered its wings inside Dinah's chest. Cousin Annabelle hadn't been the biggest part in *Caddie Woodlawn*, but it had been the best. Dinah had made it the best.

"Do you really think so?"

"I know so." Tom missed the next basket, but caught the ball as it glanced off the rim. "So what about this fight with Suzy? Can you make it up?"

Dinah shook her head. "I don't think so. We're both pretty mad. In fact, I'd better get going before she gets home from her lesson."

"Okay," Tom said. "Break a leg."

Dinah knew that was what theater people said to wish each other luck before a performance.

"And remember, Vee-Gee Two. There are no small parts, just small players. Knock 'em dead!"

Dinah ran home, her curls streaming behind her. She loved Tom, she really did. And maybe, just maybe, he was right about the play. Maybe even Village Girl Number Two could steal the show.

———

The play was scheduled for Friday, at two. On Wednesday and Thursday Mrs. Hall devoted the whole afternoon to rehearsals—dress rehearsals, she called them, in which the actors wore the same costumes they would wear in the actual play. Dinah liked her costume for Village Girl Number Two: a long old-fashioned-looking dress with full ruffled petticoats that peeked out underneath when she twirled in front of the mirror. It would have been fun to live a century ago and wear petticoats like that every day.

During the dress rehearsals, Dinah acted the part of Village Girl Number Two the way she always had. She sat quietly at her desk in the classroom scene while Tom, Becky, and Mr. Dobbins spoke their lines. She said her own six syllables, "Becky's sweet on To-om!" with lively expression, but then faded into the background again. In the closing scene she waved a small American flag along with all the other village children, an inconspicuous member of a larger crowd.

But at home, in her room, in secret, Dinah practiced a different Village Girl Number Two, one no audience could ignore. This Village Girl Number Two was going to make her short time onstage so memorable that the audience would have eyes for her alone. She imagined the roar of laughter and applause as she ran out for her curtsey at the end of the show, drowning out the applause for Tom and Becky. In one version of her daydream there was a Hollywood talent scout in the audience, looking for an unknown young actress to star in his next blockbuster film. He carefully observes Becky and Aunt Polly, even Village Girls Number One and Three. But one performance makes him leap to his feet, cheering, contract in hand: Village Girl Number Two!

Dinah's parents weren't going to the play. When she hadn't been cast as Becky or Polly, Dinah had told them not to bother. Somewhat to her chagrin, they had agreed without a protest.

"Don't come," she had told them. "I mean, it's humiliating to have your parents come to hear you say four words. Having you there would make me feel even worse."

"Well, if you're sure you don't want us . . ." her father had said. "I have to admit I could use the time at the store." And Dinah's mother had seemed relieved not to have to risk upsetting Benjamin.

But now that Village Girl Number Two was turning out to be practically a starring role, Dinah felt annoyed that her parents had opted out of attending so eagerly. They should have insisted on coming, however small her part, especially given all the fuss they made over Benjamin, who couldn't speak any lines at all. Dinah was going to write her own sibling-rivalry book someday. In it she'd tell parents, "If you're going to make a big fuss over the baby for *nothing*, then you have to make at least half as big a fuss over your other child for *something*." Of course, at the time Dinah hadn't realized how big a something Village Girl Number Two could be.

Mrs. Hall didn't even try to teach math or spelling on Friday morning. Instead she showed a nature film, for science, and played the record from a musical version of *The Adventures of Huckleberry Finn*. There would have been time for one last rehearsal, but Mrs. Hall told the class they had rehearsed the play enough. Now they had to save their energy and enthusiasm for the performance itself.

After lunch, those in the cast put on their costumes, and Mrs. Hall helped them apply real theatrical makeup. The kids in charge of props made one last trip to the auditorium to make sure that everything was in place backstage: Tom's whitewashing bucket, Aunt Polly's bottle of tonic, Mr. Dobbins's switch. Over the school's P.A. system came the call for the fourth, fifth, and sixth graders to report to the auditorium. Eight classes, plus the Room 5A parents, would be in the audience when the curtain rose on *The Adventures of Tom Sawyer*.

Beneath her rouged cheeks, Suzanne was pale with stage fright. Dinah heard her repeating her lines under her breath. But Dinah wasn't afraid of the spotlight. She could hardly wait for the classroom scene.

"All right, troupers," Mrs. Hall said, when the last-minute preparations were complete and the cast was assembled backstage in the wings. "You've worked very hard, and I'm proud of you all. Now let's get on with the show!"

Artie, as Tom Sawyer, took his place alone on the stage, in front of Aunt Polly's board fence, with a bucket of whitewash beside him.

The curtain went up. The play had begun.

The classroom scene came halfway through the play. At a signal from Mrs. Hall, the boy playing Mr. Dobbins rang the school bell, and the village children ran onstage to take their places. Dinah popped into her mouth the generous wad of bubble gum she had purchased for the occasion. Village Girl Number Two, she had decided, was fond of bubble gum.

As Mr. Dobbins addressed the class, Dinah chewed gum with all her might. She tipped back luxuriously in her chair and swung her feet up on her desk, chewing with the loud smacking sounds teachers hated. As the other village girls watched, appalled, she blew an enormous bubble. Then she sucked the gum back in with a resounding *pop*, and blew another.

A wave of laughter swept the auditorium, although no one onstage had said anything particularly funny. Dinah knew the laughter was for her. In response, she blew a third bubble, even bigger than the other two. The laughter now was loud enough that Artie and Suzanne had to raise their voices to be heard above it.

Mr. Dobbins left the room. It was time for Village Girl Number Two to say her line.

"Becky's sweet on To-om!"

Although the script didn't call for it, Dinah jumped up and ran over to the chalkboard in front of the schoolroom. She grabbed a piece of chalk and drew a big heart, with T.S. + B.T. written inside. Then she struck a lovesick pose, batting her eyes and pretending to swoon.

Village Boy Number Two had the line that followed, but, busy watching Dinah's unexpected antics, he forgot to say it. Since his line was the cue for Mr. Dobbins to return, there was an awkward pause. Nothing happened. Village Boy Number Two didn't speak. Mr. Dobbins didn't enter. Even Tony Turner, the boy in charge of prompting from the wings, was so confused that he lost his place in the script.

Somebody had to do something.

"Yoo-hoo!" Dinah called. "Oh, Mr. Dobbins! Yoo-hoo!" The yoo-hoo turned itself into a yodel: "Yoo-doo-lay-dee-hoo!" The boys in the audience whistled and stamped their feet.

Mr. Dobbins stumbled back onstage, looking confused. He flubbed his next line, but it hardly mattered. No one was listening to him, anyway. Everyone was watching Village Girl Number Two. Dinah's daydream had come true.

Somehow the scene drew to an end. As Dinah made her exit with the other village children, she half expected the Hollywood talent scout to pounce on her in the wings. But Mrs. Hall pounced instead.

"What do you think you're doing?" she demanded in a furious whisper.

Dinah thought the answer should have been obvious: stealing the show. But apparently Mrs. Hall had never heard the saying about no small parts, only small players. She looked as if she wanted to give Dinah a good shaking.

"They liked it," Dinah said, defensive. "Didn't you hear them laugh?"

"Sit there," Mrs. Hall hissed, pointing to a chair by her side. "And stay there until I say you can move. I'm not going to let you ruin the rest of the play, too."

"But I have to go on for the last scene!" Dinah had practiced some extremely amusing flag-waving routines.

"No, you don't. I think we've had quite enough of you today. More than enough."

Dinah sat where Mrs. Hall had told her to. She tried

to hold fast to the memory of the cheering audience, cheering for *her*, but the teacher's reaction to her stunning success spoiled some of her pleasure in it.

From where she sat, Dinah could see Tom and Becky alone onstage. It fell to Becky to say the closing line of the scene, one of her best lines in the play. Tom has taken the blame for the page Becky tore by mistake in Mr. Dobbins's favorite book—the blame, and a whipping, too. Becky then turns to Tom and breathes, "Tom, how *could* you be so noble!"

At least that was what Becky was supposed to say. Onstage Suzanne stood stock-still, flustered completely by the chaotic finish to the scene, her mouth opening and shutting like a fish out of water.

"Tom, how *could* you be so noble!" Tony Turner hissed from offstage, prompting her.

Suzanne just stood there, in a daze.

"Tom, how *could* you be so noble!" Tony called out, louder this time.

The audience, hearing every word, began laughing.

"Tom, how could you be so noble," Suzanne repeated woodenly. Then she buried her face in her hands and fled offstage.

Nine

In the wings, Mrs. Hall put her arm around Suzanne to comfort her. "Sit down, take a few deep breaths, and concentrate on what you have to do next," Dinah heard Mrs. Hall tell Suzanne. Becky wasn't in the next two scenes. She wasn't to appear again until the cave scene toward the end of the play. "You'll do just fine, I know you will."

The teacher led Suzanne to another folding chair a few feet away from where Dinah sat, a prisoner. Dinah hoped Suzanne wouldn't see her there, but Suzanne did.

"How could you?" Suzanne asked in a voice that trembled with rage and disappointment. "You knew how much the play meant to me. How could you spoil it?"

Dinah didn't know how to answer. Watching Suzanne's worst nightmare come true had given her a wrenching pain in her stomach, like her fake stomach leprosy, only real this time. And it had all been her fault. There was no way she could pretend that it hadn't been.

"You wanted me to forget my lines, didn't you?"

"No, I didn't. I just wanted—" How could she explain? Of course she hadn't wanted Suzanne to forget her lines. She had just wanted to be, well, important again, not an ordinary village girl, but a star.

"Never mind," Suzanne said. "It doesn't matter now."

I'm sorry. Dinah thought the words, but she didn't say them out loud.

Suzanne stood up and shook out the petticoats of her Becky Thatcher costume. "But let me tell you this, Dinah Seabrooke," she said. "You aren't going to spoil the rest of the play for me. You're not. I'm not going to let you."

"Ready, Suzanne?" Mrs. Hall asked, coming up behind her. "You're on."

"I'm ready." Suzanne smoothed back her hair and marched out onstage. And something inside Dinah wanted to cheer, "Way to go, Suzanne!"

Not that Dinah had any chance of spoiling the rest of the play, confined as she was to her chair in the wings. Alone in the shadows, she watched the cave scene as if for the first time. During rehearsals she had been busy with her various ailments, and when she had tried to listen, all she could hear was the sound of her own voice, saying Becky's lines over and over again in her imagination. Now she found herself caught up in the drama of the play in spite of herself. She was watching not Artie and Suzanne, but Tom and Becky, caring about what happened to them. Would they get out of the cave alive?

The realization struck her like a blow: Suzanne was good. Suzanne was a wonderful Becky. The admission seized Dinah before she could stop it: better than *she* would have been.

The closing scene of *The Adventures of Tom Sawyer* was performed without any flamboyant flag-waving by Village Girl Number Two. True to her word, Mrs. Hall refused to let Dinah join the others onstage. Nor did she relent when the rest of the cast ran out for their curtain call. Dinah could hear the roar of applause for Huck and Aunt Polly, Becky and Tom. There was none for Village Girl Number Two, whose efforts to steal the show had come so close to ruining it altogether.

After the play, the visiting parents came up to Room 5A for the cast party. Dinah lingered by the refreshment table as most of the parents crowded around Artie and Suzanne, just as, after other plays, they had crowded around her.

She saw Mrs. Kelly heading toward the punch bowl and pretended to be busy arranging the paper cups in neat rows on the table. Wouldn't Mrs. Kelly be mad at her for stealing the classroom scene away from Suzanne? How could the Kellys like someone who had made Suzanne forget her lines?

But Mrs. Kelly reached over the table to give Dinah

a hug and kiss. "My poor child," she said, holding her close for an instant before letting her go. Dinah wanted to burst into tears right then. Mrs. Kelly's kindness made her feel worse than a scolding would have.

At last, when Dinah couldn't bear the cast party another minute, the afternoon bell sounded. No released prisoner, free after fifty years of bread and water in solitary confinement, could have been more grateful for escape. The play was over, over forever!

Still in costume, Dinah raced home as if the whole cast of *Tom Sawyer* were chasing after her. She was glad now—so very glad!—that she had told her parents not to come to the play. They might have had questions—angry questions—about her performance as Vee-Gee Two that she wouldn't have known quite how to answer.

When Dinah reached home, she could hear her mother upstairs talking to someone on the phone. Benjamin was apparently sleeping. So far, so good. But, foraging in the kitchen for a snack, Dinah could tell that her mother wasn't having a good day. The breakfast dishes still sat on the counter, bits of milk-soaked Grape-Nuts hardened to rocklike encrustations in the bottom of the cereal bowls. Dinah had thought about rinsing hers and setting it in the sink, but in the excitement about the play she hadn't actually gotten around to *doing* it. The garbage pail under the sink smelled as if its contents should have been taken out yesterday, if not the day before. Unopened, the morning paper, rolled up in its plastic bag, lay on the floor.

On the kitchen table, next to the day's mail all in a

jumble, sat Mrs. Seabrooke's To Do list. At the top of the page, as if to cheer herself on, Dinah's mother had printed, "Today is the first day of the rest of your life!" The list had twenty-three items on it, some starred as high-priority tasks. Not a single item was crossed off.

Guilt-stricken—hadn't Dinah promised that she would help more around the house?—Dinah began gathering the breakfast dishes and carrying them to the sink. If she could take care of at least one job on the list, that would leave only twenty-two for her mother to worry about.

She had almost finished loading the dishwasher when she heard her mother come into the kitchen behind her.

"Ta-dah!" Dinah whirled around to display her good work.

But her mother looked angry.

"Item number one," Dinah explained, since her mother didn't seem to get it. "On your To Do list. Done!"

"Never mind the dishes," her mother said. "Sit down. I have to talk to you. The phone call I was on upstairs? That was Mrs. Hall."

Mrs. Hall! In her relief that the play was finally over, Dinah had forgotten that Mrs. Hall was sure to call. Dinah was used to having teachers call her parents, but not for something like this. Other phone calls had concerned various amusing additions to Dinah's Permanent Record. She didn't mind a phone call home about dancing on the rooftop in the rain. But this time—she didn't want her parents to know about the play. She just didn't.

"How could you?" Dinah's mother asked, as if she had been eavesdropping on Dinah's conversation with Suzanne, echoing Suzanne's same question. "Suzanne's your friend, your best friend. Isn't she entitled to some attention once in her life, without your trying to steal it away from her?"

Dinah already felt terrible and horrible and miserable about what she had done to the play. How much worse was she expected to feel?

"I guess so, but—"

"You've been moping around the house ever since Suzanne got the part, and let me tell you, your father and I haven't liked it one bit. Of course it was a disappointment to you at first, and we sympathized, you know we did. But, really, Dinah, this is too much. Poor Suzanne!"

Something in Dinah snapped. Suzanne was hardly the only one who had suffered because of the play. "Poor *Suzanne*? She got to be Becky."

"That's right. For the first time in—how many? three?— years, she got something and you didn't."

Not just *something*—the best part in the play, the part Dinah had wanted with all her heart.

"You seem to think you have a claim on everybody's attention, all the time. But Suzanne deserves some attention, too, and the other kids in the play. And so does Benjamin."

"Benjamin?" This was too much. "Benjamin gets *all* the attention."

"That's not true, Dinah. It's just not true. I admit a

newborn infant is very demanding, but look at it this way. For ten years our whole world revolved around you. Now it has to revolve around both of you."

"You didn't come to the play," Dinah muttered, turning away so her mother wouldn't see how close she was to crying.

"You told us *not* to come," her mother said wearily. "If you had wanted us to be there, one of us would have come, and you know it."

"*One* of you."

"Yes, and one of us would have stayed with Benjamin. I don't know, Dinah. Maybe your father and I made a mistake not having a second child sooner, but this is how the timing worked out. We didn't mean to spoil you."

Spoil. It was a horrid word. It made Dinah feel like a piece of bruised fruit, an apple with brown, rotting spots on it, left, unwanted, in the bottom of the crisper.

From upstairs came an all-too-familiar cry. Wah, wah, wah! Dinah was sick of the sound of it. Wah, wah, wah! For the first time Dinah almost hated Benjamin. She turned to go outside, to flee up the hill to the park, as far away from that *noise* as she could go.

"No, you don't," her mother said. "I'm going to feed Benjamin, and then you're going to take him for a walk. It's high time I got some help around here, and, starting today, I'm going to."

Her mother was gone. Mechanically, Dinah measured detergent into the dishwasher and started the wash cycle. Her mother hadn't even thanked her for helping with the dishes. To keep herself from thinking, from feeling, Dinah began wiping the counters with a damp paper towel. From now on, apparently, she would be an unpaid, unloved household drudge, like Cinderella, washing dishes, wiping counters, pushing strollers, maybe even scrubbing floors on her hands and knees. Her mother was probably sorry they didn't have any ashes for her to sit in. Maybe they could send her over to crouch by the Kellys' big kitchen fireplace, a soot-streaked scullery maid watching while Suzanne got ready to go to the ball.

"Here he is," Dinah's mother announced, coming back to the kitchen with Benjamin in her arms. "Take him out for forty-five minutes or so. The stroller's on the porch."

Benjamin smiled up at Dinah when she took him, but she didn't smile back.

Outside it was warm and humid, the sky like gray gauze, close and damp. Dinah marched up the hill, pushing the stroller ahead of her with hard, angry jerks, glad when she bumped it over a broken stretch of concrete. She didn't linger at the park, but turned around to head back down the hill again. Her mother probably didn't want her to have any rest. Up and down, up and down! That's what her mother wanted. It was what Cinderella's stepmother would have wanted, too.

It was easier going down the hill, but Dinah made it harder by pushing the stroller as fast as she could. She imagined her mother watching from the window with a stopwatch in her hand. *Hurry it up, lazybones! When*

I say fast, I mean FAST! She didn't look to the left or right. This wasn't supposed to be a sightseeing tour. It was supposed to be drudgery.

Faster! Faster! It was all Dinah could do to keep the stroller from flying down the hill of its own accord. What if Dinah, the all-purpose drudge, ended up setting a world stroller-pushing record? Ha! That would serve her mother right. Think of the attention Dinah would get then. The flashbulbs popping, the talk-show interviews, the newspaper headlines—GIRL, TEN, SETS STROLLER RECORD. And, in smaller print underneath, PARENTS FURIOUS AT HER SUCCESS.

They were almost home when Dinah caught her foot on an uneven piece of pavement. She let go of the handle, just for an instant, but when she tried to grab it back again, the stroller was gone, hurtling down the sidewalk, over the curb, into the cross street below.

And then Dinah saw the approaching car.

Ten

Dinah closed her eyes. She heard the hysterical, drawn-out screech of car brakes. "Oh, my God," a man said. A cry, unmistakably Benjamin's. Benjamin couldn't cry if he were—

Dinah opened her eyes and started running. She had to get to Benjamin, to pick him up and hold him tight and never let him go. "Benjamin, I'm coming! Oh, Benjamin!"

The car had skidded up onto the grass, leaving a black trail of scorched rubber across the road, but it had stopped in time. On the far side of Tulip Street lay Benjamin's stroller, knocked onto its side where it had struck the curb. Because Dinah had remembered to fasten his little seatbelt, Benjamin hadn't fallen out. Held fast by the belt, he lay sideways in the overturned stroller, wailing in fear and indignation.

Dinah groped at the seatbelt clasp, but couldn't see for her tears.

"Let me." The driver of the car, a middle-aged man wearing a business suit, knelt down beside the stroller. "Here we go, little fella," he said.

"Give him to me," Dinah begged.

There. Dinah nestled Benjamin against her shoulder, enfolding him with crossed arms. His ragged, quivering sobs quieted as she soothed him.

"It's all right, Benjamin," she crooned. "Dinah has you now. It's all right."

Then Dinah's mother was there, and her father, too, home from the store early that day, and some of the neighbors. The driver of the car, clearly shaken, explained how Benjamin's stroller had appeared out of nowhere, flying unescorted into the street.

"And I thought, Oh, my God, I'm not going to be able to stop. Another foot, and . . ." His voice trailed away.

"Dinah?" her father asked gently.

She tried to remember. It seemed so long ago. "I was pushing it too fast. And I tripped. And it was—" She felt the horror of the moment, when she had lunged for the stroller handle, and it hadn't been there. "Gone," she whispered.

Dinah's mother took Benjamin now, and her father

drew Dinah into his embrace. Dinah's mother reached out a hand to stroke Dinah's sweat-dampened curls. Somehow, unbelievably, they weren't angry with her. This was a hundred, a thousand, a million billion times worse than the play, but this time they weren't angry. Maybe the enormity of what had almost happened put them beyond any feelings except thanksgiving and relief. Or maybe this time they knew their anger would be nothing compared to what Dinah herself already felt.

For supper, Dinah's father made scrambled eggs and toast. The eggs were too runny, but nobody cared. Dinah did the dishes, even cleaning the horrible, slippery eggy bits out of the drain in the sink. Then she escaped to her room and closed the door behind her.

GENIUS AT WORK—EMPLOYEES ONLY, it said on the door. But Dinah was no genius. Right then she wasn't even somebody she liked. The attention-grabbing antics of Vee-Gee Two, Suzanne's outburst backstage at the play, the fight with her mother, the near tragedy from Dinah's imaginary stroller-pushing contest—all the memories of the day crowded together and overwhelmed her. *How could you?* Suzanne had asked. *How could you?* her mother had echoed.

Dinah didn't know. But alone in her room, sitting cross-legged in the middle of her bed, she made a solemn vow: She would never ever seek the spotlight again.

All her troubles had come from trying to get attention. She had thought she deserved extra attention for being, well, more interesting than everybody else. It had seemed only fair and reasonable to her that she should be onstage while other people were in the audience, that she should talk while other people listened. But right that minute Dinah was sick to death of herself.

How selfish could one person be? Why should she—why should *anybody*—get all the attention all the time? It was beginning to dawn on Dinah that the way she felt about herself was the way that other people felt about *themselves*. Everybody wanted attention. Dinah had just been more greedy about it, grabbing more than her share. Her hogging the spotlight had hurt Suzanne deeply and cost Dinah their friendship. For her antics with Benjamin's stroller, Dinah had almost paid an unbearable price.

"I will never ever seek the spotlight again. I will never clown around while pushing a stroller. I will never try to make my part in a play better than everybody else's." The list grew longer and longer. "I will never try to recite the longest poem. I will never eat fourteen Dixie cups of ice cream. I will never talk about myself and not listen when the other person talks. I won't steal the show. I won't show off. I won't brag. I won't add things to my Permanent Record."

The next one stuck in her throat. Dinah made herself say it: "I will never again dance on the rooftop in the rain."

At seven-thirty in the evening, exhausted, Dinah crawled under the covers and fell asleep.

———

Dinah was up and dressed Saturday morning while the rest of the family, Benjamin included, was still sleeping. She was seized by the urge to do something noble and useful. If only there had been a blizzard overnight, she could shovel four feet of drifted snow from the walks and driveway! But snow shoveling was hardly a noble and useful possibility for a late April morning.

The laundry hamper in the bathroom was full. Could Dinah surprise her parents by having four loads of wash out on the line before breakfast? No. Dinah had never used the washing machine, and she had read stories about the disasters that befell children using the washing machine for the first time. In one, all the family's clothes turned a pale purple. In another, the machine failed to turn off, and the house was flooded with a rising sea of soapsuds. Dinah didn't want to swell the ranks of such unfortunate adventurers.

Suzanne could make coffee for her parents in their Mr. Coffee machine. Suzanne could even grind up the coffee beans. But Dinah had never watched Suzanne do it, and she didn't know if the Seabrookes' coffee maker worked the same way as Mr. Coffee.

Finally Dinah gathered together all her change. She'd ride her bike to the twenty-four-hour doughnut shop near Hazlewood School and buy a dozen doughnuts for a breakfast treat.

"Doughnuts," her mother said, nursing Benjamin in the living room when Dinah returned. "What a lovely idea."

"Doughnuts?" Mr. Seabrooke asked, coming downstairs still in his robe and pajamas. "Did somebody say doughnuts?"

Dinah poured three glasses of milk and passed out paper napkins, and they all ate doughnuts in the living room. It was the first time Dinah could remember eating in the living room. Her mother generally didn't allow it; she said it made crumbs. But now the living room was untidy enough that a few crumbs didn't matter.

"I wanted to do the laundry," Dinah said, "but I didn't know how."

"I'll show you after breakfast," her mother promised. "I don't know why I never showed you before. I guess I never needed to. I was always so—"

"Organized," Dinah and her father finished together.

"But you know what?" Mrs. Seabrooke bit deep into a jelly-filled cruller. "I'm beginning to think sometimes a person can be *too* organized. Sometimes you might as well give up, and throw away your To Do lists, and just *be*. What do you say, Benjamin?"

She sat him up on her lap, and he looked wise and serious, as if he were considering the question from every conceivable angle. Then he gave an enormous, heartfelt, satisfying burp.

"He agrees," Mr. Seabrooke said. "You and me both, Benjamin."

———

Dinah's mother noticed it first. A few days later, she asked Dinah out of the blue, "Are you feeling all right, honey?"

"Uh-huh. Why?"

"I don't know. You've been so quiet lately. We've hardly heard a peep out of you."

Dinah knew the answer to that one. "Peep," she said.

Her mother laughed, but she still looked concerned. "Is anything bothering you at school?"

"No, except—"

"Except for your fight with Suzanne. Really, kids can be so stubborn. Just make it up, why don't you? Just let her know you're sorry. Suzanne's not the kind of girl who holds a grudge. I bet she wants to be friends again as badly as you do."

Dinah shook her head. She knew Suzanne wouldn't forgive her for all that had happened, and she didn't blame her.

But Dinah wasn't quiet these days because of her quarrel with Suzanne, though that was a dull ache in her heart. She was trying with all her might to be less selfish, to talk less and listen more. She was making a conscious effort not to regale the world with her stories. And, actually, there hadn't been any stories to tell: no stunts, no juggling, no pies in the face. Just—nothing.

Mrs. Hall noticed it, too. A week after the play, she called Dinah to her desk during Silent Reading.

"Dinah, I have to say I'm very pleased with the improvement in your attitude. I haven't had to reprimand you once this week. It makes my job a lot more pleasant when I can be a teacher instead of a disciplinarian."

Dinah didn't say anything, but she felt a little pang of longing for the old crowd-pleasing, show-stopping Dynamite Dinah who was no more. Didn't Mrs. Hall miss the old Dinah just a little tiny teensy-weensy bit?

"But what I wanted to talk to you about, Dinah,

is our schoolwide spring talent assemblies. This is a new program we're trying this year. Every teacher is going to be selecting two of his or her students, who will then perform at an assembly for all the classes in that grade.

"I haven't yet chosen the person for Room 5A's second slot, but for the first naturally I thought of you. I'd like you to represent us by giving your recitation of 'Renascence' one more time."

Every once in a while the universe surprised Dinah by surpassing even her own most pleasing daydreams.

"I know you'll do a lovely job, Dinah. At first I wasn't sure I should choose you, because of what you did during *The Adventures of Tom Sawyer*. But I've been impressed with your behavior this past week, and I've decided not to hold that incident against you. So, what do you say, Dinah?"

Dinah swallowed hard. In her first rush of excitement, she had forgotten that she was never ever *ever* going to seek the spotlight again.

"Actually," she began. Oh, it was hard, too hard! "Actually, I'd rather not."

Mrs. Hall, who had taken off her glasses to wipe a speck of lint from one lens, put them on again. "You'd rather *not*?"

"I'd rather not."

"May I ask why?"

Dinah shook her head.

"Oh, Dinah," Mrs. Hall said. "It's all or nothing with

you, isn't it? There isn't any halfway, any meeting in the middle. All right, go sit down."

Dinah sat down.

———

Giving up the talent show was the hardest thing Dinah had ever done, and no one, except Mrs. Hall, even knew she had done it. If only she could tell Suzanne, see, I gave up the talent show, and I did it to make up for the play, because I'm sorry, really, truly sorry, about what I did.

Suddenly it struck Dinah that she had never actually apologized to Suzanne for anything that had happened. She had never said out loud the words *I'm sorry.* She had said them so often to herself, over and over again, that it seemed to Dinah that she had done nothing but apologize from morning till night. But naturally it wouldn't seem that way to Suzanne.

It should be so easy to say those two little words, but Dinah could hardly bear the thought of saying them straight out, to Suzanne's face. Saying them wasn't the problem. The problem was waiting to hear what Suzanne would say in return. What if she turned on her heel and swept coldly away? What if she said, *Sorry isn't good enough*? Or, worst of all, *Don't think this makes us friends again, because it doesn't.*

Still, the words had to be said, and Dinah had to say them. She'd write Suzanne a note—that was what she'd do—and leave it in Suzanne's desk with a bag of M&M's.

On Monday morning, when Suzanne was at the chalk-board, Dinah slipped her apology and peace offering into Suzanne's desk. She waited for Suzanne to find them when she sat down again, but Suzanne settled back to work without first checking inside her desk for possible hidden surprises. It was worse than waiting for Mrs. Hall to read the cast list for a play.

Then, after lunch, when Dinah reached into her desk for her social studies textbook, she felt a familiar object—the same bag of M&M's she had left for Suzanne. Tears stung Dinah's eyes. Suzanne had given the candy back to her. She could hardly have said more plainly that she didn't want to be friends.

But the bag felt different, lighter. It had been opened and then folded shut again. And there was a note taped to its side.

Dinah made herself read it:

> *Dear Dinah,*
>   *I saved the red, orange, and yellow ones for you.*
>
>   *Love,*
>   *Suzanne*

Eleven

It was as if they had never not been friends.

"Should we go to your house or mine?" Suzanne asked Dinah after school.

"Yours," Dinah answered promptly. Her nostrils yearned for the woodsy smell of the Kellys' kitchen.

"But I need to see *Benjamin*," Suzanne almost wailed. "I have to see him smile."

"Both, then," Dinah said.

They reached Suzanne's house first. Tom's face lit up with a wide grin when Dinah burst into the kitchen. "There she is," he sang to the tune for the Miss America pageant. "Mi-iss Dynamite!"

Dinah flushed with pleasure. Even if she wasn't Dynamite Dinah any more.

"What's up, Dynamite?" Tom straddled a straight-backed wooden chair by the fireplace and waited for the predictable avalanche of stories. This part was going to be hard, as hard as giving up the talent show.

"Nothing," Dinah said.

"Nothing? How's the old Permanent Record?"

"It's the same."

"No new additions?"

Dinah shook her head. She had made a vow and was going to stick by it.

"Listen," Tom said, lowering his voice so the others wouldn't hear. "About the play. I gave you a bum steer with all that business about small parts and small players. I guess I feel kind of responsible for what happened next."

"It wasn't your fault," Dinah said. "You said that Village Girl Number Two could be a good part, not that it could be the best part in the whole play. I just got carried away."

Tom looked relieved. "I mean it, Dinah, a guy's got to be careful what he says around you. You get an idea in your head, and it's like a lighted match around—well, around dynamite."

At Dinah's house, Mrs. Seabrooke seemed as glad to see Suzanne as Tom had been to see Dinah, although she didn't express her sentiments musically.

"Suzanne! We don't have M&M's today, but how about—" She surveyed the contents of the half-empty refrigerator. "We don't have much of anything, I'm afraid."

"All I want is Benjamin," Suzanne said.

"Benjamin we have."

Suzanne scooped him up from his baby carrier on the kitchen table. "Can you smile?" she coaxed him. "Can you give me one teensy-weensy little—He smiled! Look, he smiled!"

It was worth it, being friends again, even if Dinah had to give up the spotlight forever.

On Saturday, the girls baked cookies at Suzanne's house—oatmeal cookies with chocolate chips *and* nuts *and* raisins, the kind with just enough cookie dough to hold everything else together. On Sunday, they helped Dinah's father wash the Seabrookes' two cars. The day was hot and sunny, and the spray from the hose was sparkling and cold. Now that Dinah was no longer going to be an actress, she might seriously consider a career at a car wash. There were few things in life nicer than swishing soapsuds on a dirty, dusty Honda Civic and watching it come clean again. And it would be fun to have an excuse to play all day long with a garden hose.

In the old days—just barely a week ago?—the hose would have served as a splendid comic prop. Dinah could imagine an entire circus act built around hoses. But now she contented herself with spraying the Honda and, only occasionally, dousing Suzanne.

It wasn't too bad, really, to pass up chances for attention and applause. The world still had springtime in it, and Benjamin, and fresh-baked cookies, and a pos-

109

sible future car-washing career. And yet Dinah felt somehow sorry for the world, deprived of humorous routines with her hose, denied the opportunity to hear another recitation of "Renascence." And despite everything that had happened, deep down she felt sorry for herself, too. She was nicer than she had been before, yes, but undeniably less interesting.

Then, early Monday morning, looking through her drawer for a rubber band, Dinah came upon her old false nose. It was an extremely realistic one, a big bulbous red nose with glassless wire frames above and a bushy black mustache beneath. She had worn it a lot that past summer, but by mid-August she had tired of it and put it away. No one at school, except Suzanne, had seen her in it.

Dinah knew she should shut the drawer right then and take a rubber band from the jar her mother kept in the pantry. But she had to try the nose on, just once, for old-time's sake. When she did, she felt the same tingle of excitement she remembered from the summer before.

She tucked the nose into her backpack and headed off to school. There was no harm in having a false nose in your backpack, as long as you didn't actually wear it.

"Guess who has a substitute?" Artie greeted her on the playground. "And guess who it is."

"Not Mrs. Overton."

"You guessed it!"

No. She wouldn't even think about wearing her false nose. Not even to confuse and confound Mrs. Overton.

In line, waiting for the bell, Dinah poked Suzanne.

"Look what I found this morning." She unzipped her backpack far enough for Suzanne to peek inside.

"Oh, Dinah! Put it on!"

"Not at school."

"But you looked so funny in it." Suzanne burst out laughing at the memory.

"What are you guys laughing at?" Artie, behind them in line, wanted to know.

"Nothing."

"Dinah has this wonderful fake nose. It's the best one I've ever seen."

"Let's see. Put it on."

"No. I don't want to."

"*I'll* put it on. Give it here."

"Okay, I'll wear it," Dinah said hastily. "Close your eyes."

Artie and Suzanne obeyed. Dinah fastened on the nose. It had an elastic cord that slipped over her ears and under her hair.

"You can open them now."

Suzanne went into a gale of giggles.

"All right, Dinah!" Artie said approvingly. "Hey, Nathan, look at Dinah's nose!"

Half of Room 5A craned their necks to see. Dinah soaked up their laughter like a parched cornfield after a month-long drought, welcoming the first rain. She could never get enough of it.

"Dinah, the red-nosed reindeer!" Nathan sang.

"Who knows? The nose knows!" Artie intoned in a deep voice.

The bell rang. Her nose flaming, her mustache bristling, Dinah walked with her class down the hall to Room 5A.

There was Mrs. Overton, as plump and grandmotherly as ever. Dinah held her breath, but Mrs. Overton was too busy with the flag salute and roll call to notice any unusual noses in the classroom. She made all the same mistakes with the children's names that she had made before. But this time Suzanne answered herself when her name was called.

Finally, "Dinah Seabrooke," Mrs. Overton read from the list.

Everyone laughed. Mrs. Overton looked up.

"Dinah Seabrooke?" Then she saw the nose. "All right, enough of that. I remember *you* from last time."

Dinah sat innocently, as if she didn't understand what Mrs. Overton was talking about.

"The nose," Mrs. Overton said. "Take it off."

"It doesn't come off."

More laughter.

"It doesn't *come* off?"

"I've been sick," Dinah explained. "Really sick. I'm better now, but the sickness made my nose turn big and red. And it made me grow a mustache. And now I have to wear glasses."

Mrs. Overton hesitated. Dinah maintained her look of injured innocence. If Mrs. Overton believed her, she could die right then, happy.

"I meant what I said, young lady." Dinah would have

to go on living. "Or else you can march down and tell your story to Mr. Saganario."

Dinah removed her nose, with some regret. It would have made such a nice entry for her Permanent Record: *Today in class Dinah refused to remove her false nose and mustache.* Of course, she wasn't supposed to care about her Permanent Record anymore. But Dinah banished any thoughts of her broken vow.

"That's better. Where were we? Anthony Turner."

Mrs. Hall would have confiscated the nose, for the day at least and maybe for the remainder of the school year. Before that idea could occur to Mrs. Overton, Dinah whisked her nose back into her backpack.

She took her backpack with her when the class was dismissed for lunch. This time she needed no urging from Artie or Suzanne. As soon as she reached the cafeteria line, the nose was in place again. The cafeteria workers, more broad-minded than Mrs. Overton, broke into big grins when they saw her. Why *not* wear a false nose if it brightened someone else's day? It would have been selfish of Dinah *not* to.

Dinah had to take off the nose to eat her Beefaroni. She didn't want to get tomato sauce on her mustache. But she put it back on as soon as she had finished. She was surprised that more people didn't wear false noses. She imagined advertisements for false noses, on the model of the American Express card commercials: Don't leave home without one.

Across the room, a lower grader dropped his tray,

sending Beefaroni, coleslaw, and milk crashing to the floor. When Pop Fody arrived with his mop, Dinah could hardly believe that she hadn't noticed the resemblance before. Pop Fody had wire glasses, an oversized nose, and a big black mustache. With her matching set, Dinah looked like a miniature version of Pop. She could pass for his daughter, if he had one—Popparina.

As Pop mopped, Dinah stole across the room, holding her hands in front of her face to hide her nose from view. When she was right behind Pop, she took her hands away. Ta-dah!

The cafeteria was suddenly silent.

Pop turned around. For a long moment Pop and Popparina stood facing each other. Had Dinah gone too far again?

Then Pop began to laugh. Dinah laughed, too. And all of first-period lunch laughed with them.

Dinah knew that that was a once-in-a-lifetime triumph, a moment that could not be topped. Suzanne was still laughing when Dinah took her seat again. But something about the way Suzanne laughed—the way she covered her face with her hands when she was laughing the hardest—made Dinah remember the terrible moment during *Tom Sawyer* when Suzanne had forgotten her best line. Feeling ashamed now, Dinah snatched off her false nose and buried it at the bottom of her backpack. Would she ever stop being Village Girl Number Two, thinking every show was hers to steal? What if she *had* hurt Pop Fody's feelings? She had been so bent on getting a laugh that, as always, she hadn't bothered to think about anyone else. Nothing had changed, after all. Dinah was still going around shouting at the world, "Yoo-hoo, world! Look at me!"

After school, Suzanne practiced for her spring piano recital, while Dinah lay on the Kellys' couch, her eyes closed, trying to think. It was the first time Dinah had heard Suzanne's recital piece, and the beauty and the ache of it mixed themselves up with Dinah's own mixed-up feelings.

"What is that? What are you playing?"

Suzanne answered without looking away from the piano. "It's called 'Poem.' By Fibich."

Dinah had a sudden realization. "Suzanne!"

Suzanne stopped playing, her hands poised over the keys.

"You're good! At playing the piano. I mean, really good."

"I'm getting better," Suzanne acknowledged. "But I told you, I always forget my piece in the middle."

"That doesn't matter. What does your teacher say? Does she think you're good?"

"I guess so. She says I could be good someday if I practice hard."

Suzanne began playing again, in the middle of the piece, where she had left off.

So Suzanne had *two* talents, acting *and* music. And what about Dinah? She had a talent, too, for wearing false noses and reciting long poems—for entertaining people—but hers was a talent that brought nothing but trouble.

Dinah gave up trying to think. She signaled good-bye to Suzanne, gathered up her jacket and backpack, and started for home.

Dinah found her mother in the living room, with Benjamin half asleep in her lap. A trickle of milk ran down his chin, and he had the look of drunken contentment that always came after nursing.

"How was school today, honey?" Mrs. Seabrooke asked.

It used to be Dinah's favorite question, but it had been so long since she had a dazzling, wonderful story to tell. Today she did, but she couldn't take any pleasure in it.

"Remember my nose?" she said, anyway.

Her mother eyed Dinah's real nose, confused. "What's there to remember?"

"No, my fake nose from last summer. Well, I found it in my desk drawer this morning." The tale of the nose tumbled out.

Mrs. Seabrooke laughed, but her eyes were serious. "It must have been extremely funny," she said. "But, honey, what if you had hurt that man's feelings? Really, Dinah, you have to learn to think a little more before you clown around. You don't want to repeat your experience at the play—"

"I *know*," Dinah interrupted, almost fiercely. "Don't you think I know? Ever since the play I've tried, I've really tried, not to be a clown at all, not to do a single solitary funny thing. Mrs. Hall even called me up to her desk to tell me how good I've been. I've tried so hard! I mean, I almost lost being friends with Suzanne the way

I was before, and you guys were mad at me, too—and if anything had happened to Benjamin. . . . But it's hard. I see a false nose, and it's like I have to put it on. And part of me *wants* to put it on. Because, like, it really was funny, today in the cafeteria, being Popparina. So what am I going to do?"

Mrs. Seabrooke reached for a receiving blanket to cover Benjamin. Then she took Dinah's hand. "Dinah, listen to me. You're an entertainer. That's part of who you are. Ever since you were a baby hardly older than Benjamin, you've made your father and me laugh. There's nothing wrong with entertaining people. Whoever said that there was?"

"But there *is*. Look at all the things that happened. Or almost happened. All the bad things."

"Oh, honey, those things didn't happen because you were an entertainer. They happened because you picked the wrong time and place for entertaining. You can't put on a floor show while you're pushing a stroller. And I'm sure Mrs. Hall would like to see you do your entertaining outside of classroom hours."

"When we had our fight, do you know what Suzanne said? She said that I have only one topic, myself, and that's all I ever talk about. Like I was a selfish person, a bad person."

"Suzanne was very angry when she said that, and she had a right to be. But you know she loves your stories. She wouldn't have been your friend all these years if she hadn't thought you were basically a delightful companion. It's just that you have to let other people be entertainers sometimes, too. You have to listen to their stories, just as you want them to listen to yours."

Could it really be all right to be an entertainer, after all? Dinah felt the stirring of hope. She could make herself learn to take turns in the spotlight. And, really, when you got right down to it, there was plenty of attention in the world, enough for everyone to get some, enough for everyone to get lots. Looking back, she had liked hearing the other kids recite their poems—Nathan and Artie, Mandy and Suzanne. Once she had made herself really listen backstage at *Tom Sawyer*, she had found herself enjoying being a member of the audience. And there would be other plays. She'd have small parts in some, big parts in others. Everybody had to be a village girl sometimes. Nobody could be Becky every single time all her life long.

"I just don't want to hurt anybody else," Dinah said. In a way, that was really what it came down to.

"Don't, then!" her mother said.

"It's like, entertaining people is supposed to make them happy, not sad. That's what I want to do."

"Do it, then!" her mother said.

"I will," Dinah said, and her heart swelled with a sudden rush of joy. She felt like the girl in "Renascence," who had lost her life and had it given back to her.

———

Dinah ran all the way to school the next morning. Before the flag salute, even, she presented herself at Mrs. Hall's desk, ready with her question.

"What is it, Dinah?"

"About the talent assembly? Have you picked the two people from our class yet?"

"Not at all. I haven't made my choice for either slot."

"Is it too late for me to change my mind? Because if it isn't, I'd like to do 'Renascence' again, after all."

"It's certainly not too late. I'm glad you reconsidered, and I'd love to have you."

"And for the other slot? Well, I have an idea for that, too. Would you want someone who's a really truly talented piano player? Well, she's a really truly talented actress, too, and you already know that, but you've never heard her play the piano, and I think she's really good."

"That would be wonderful, Dinah. Who is it?"

And Dinah told her.

———

Mrs. Hall heard Suzanne play "Poem" on the piano in the school auditorium during music class the next day, and it was settled: Suzanne and Dinah would be the two representatives of Room 5A in the talent assembly.

"What if I forget it halfway through?" Suzanne asked Dinah that afternoon. They were pushing Benjamin's stroller together—very carefully—to the park at the top of the hill.

"Just use your music! No one will care. I'll turn the pages for you."

Suzanne stopped walking. "Do you ever have times when you feel, right this minute I'm completely, totally happy? Well, that's how I feel right now."

Dinah's heart came close to bursting, too. She was

going to get to recite "Renascence" again, after all, and Suzanne was going to play the piano in front of the whole school. And the azaleas were in bloom, the low bushes heavy with white and pink and deep-red blossoms. And Benjamin would be ten weeks old tomorrow.

They were at the park now, with the stroller safely parked on level ground.

"Yoo-hoo, Benjamin," Dinah called. "Look at me and Suzanne!"

Dinah still had her false nose with her in her backpack. You never knew when a false nose might come in handy. "Here," she said to Suzanne. "You wear it."

Blushing at the silliness, but obviously pleased to be asked, Suzanne put it on. With her long blond braids, the black mustache looked even funnier on Suzanne than it had on Dinah.

Benjamin smiled, a wide grin that lit up his little pumpkin face. He seemed to know that something was funny without knowing exactly what it was.

"Yoo-hoo, Benjamin! Yoo-doo-lay-dee-hoo!" Dinah yodeled.

Then, for the first time in his life on planet Earth, Benjamin laughed. It was an unmistakable, gurgling laugh of pure delight.

Enchanted, Dinah laughed with him. The more she and Suzanne laughed, the more Benjamin laughed, and the more he laughed, the more they did, all three of them giddy with laughter on a cloudless May afternoon.